MEET ME UNDER
THE MISTLETOE

USA TODAY BESTSELLING AUTHOR

STACEY KENNEDY

Print Edition

Stacey Kennedy
www.staceykennedy.com

Edited by Christa Soule
Proofread by Jolene Perry
Cover Design by Sweet 'N Spicy Designs

Manufactured in Canada

For everyone who believes
in Christmas magic.

PROLOGUE

A LITTLE SPICE and sweetness packed into a gorgeous body was going to cost Darryl Wilson his job as a camp counselor at River Rock's Wilderness Camp. A job he needed since he was paying his way through his criminal justice diploma at the college. For as long as he could remember, he wanted to be a cop. He'd always followed the rules; had a good sense of right and wrong engrained in him by his single-parent mom. But the brunette with the tight pony tails and pretty green eyes, and green camp T-shirt tied beneath her breasts—showing her midriff that he couldn't stop looking at, made him want to break every rule in his rulebook.

"You're going to get me fired," he said to Penelope, slowly striding toward her while she backed away, giving him a sexy grin. Across the lake were the cabins that housed the tweens all tucked away for the night, the nightlights in the cabins casting a warm glow out into the darkness.

"We both could get fired for this." Penelope had been hired on by the camp five days ago for the arts and crafts cabin, and there was a very strict no-fraternizing-with-staff rule.

"It's fun to live on the wild side," she practically purred, tempting him and teasing him the way she had been since she arrived, slowing walking back until she leaned against a boulder. "And I know you want me as much as I want you."

Damn did he ever. He was rock hard as he licked his lips, watching her mouth, then he took her hand and pulled her up until she stood closer to him. "You're right. I do want you." He'd never wanted anything or anyone more in his twenty years on this planet.

She nibbled her bottom lip then crossed her legs, bringing his attention to how gorgeous they were. "Then what are you waiting for? Kiss me."

His dick twitched at the blatant heat in her expression. Screw the job.

He closed the distance then pressed his lips against hers. She let out a soft moan that unraveled him as he wrapped one arm around her waist, tugging her even closer. He opened his mouth and she followed his lead, letting him have a taste of her. His other hand threaded into her hair, and she wiggled against his throbbing erection. He'd never heard of or experienced this type of *need* before. He felt every single brush of her lips until he didn't know where she began and he ended. And he was hungry. Starving, in fact, for *her*.

He forced himself to break the kiss, reminding his raging hard-on he didn't really know this girl well enough to take anything more than a kiss from her. He knew she was the cousin of the Carter sisters, Clara, Amelia, and Maisie, and that she was seventeen years old, but that was it. When he got a good look at the desire in her gaze, he had to step back so as not to grab her and make her his right then and there.

"Not bad for our first kiss," she said, breathless, pressing herself tighter against him, bringing heat and electricity pinging in the air.

Jesus Christ. "Believe me, Penelope, stick with me, and I'll make our first everything incredible." He cupped her face, overwhelmed by what he felt with her, this girl he'd only known for a handful of days. He never broke the rules. He'd never risked a job before. And no girl ever made him so turned on and so drawn in. With Penelope, everything felt different. Intense. The biggest difference between her and the other girls he'd kissed, he didn't want to let her go.

Desperate to have more of her, he sealed his mouth across hers again, and her soft needy whimper blazed heat through him. He fisted her ponytail, driven by the intensity burning between them. Every swipe of her tongue and hard press of her sweet body against his only made him want *more.* Hot, hard, and ready to take her in any and all the ways she'd allow, he drew away and then met her hooded eyes. "Damn, girl, you make me want to kiss you every day for the rest of my life."

When Darryl woke in his cabin the following morning, she was gone. For the next ten years.

CHAPTER ONE

"*HE KNOWS IF you've been bad or good...*" the long-haired brunette with the sparkling green eyes sang.

These days, not much gathered a crowd large enough to warrant a call to 911, but tonight was definitely not an ordinary night. The wrought-iron streetlights beamed soft light down on the sidewalk along River Rock's historic Main Street, revealing large snowflakes fluttering down as Officer Darryl Wilson strode up to the large fountain in the center of town. The small town nestled into the Colorado mountains saw less crime than Disneyland on any given day. There hadn't been a murder in River Rock since sometime in the 1970s, and most crime was either teenagers stirring up trouble, shady businessmen, domestic disputes, or more likely, drunk tourists getting into shenanigans. This time, just before eleven o'clock at night, the trouble was an intoxicated woman skating on the fountain in her high heels. And as he stepped closer, Darryl couldn't believe his eyes.

Penelope Carter. He'd heard she'd come back to town a few days ago, but he wasn't expecting to see her like this.

The girl who'd blown his mind at summer camp with the hottest kiss of his life when he was a camp counselor and then abruptly bailed, leaving him to never hear from her again, was skating before him. She'd been a pretty girl back then. She'd grown into a gorgeous woman with curves in all the right places that had his full attention.

"Santa Claus is coming to town," Penelope continued singing, pushing off one heel and lifting her hands in the air as if she were a figure skater and the music was real, not in her head.

Impressive, really. She skated better on heels than most people did on skates.

Darryl sighed and took in the crowd next to her with their cell phones out filming Penelope. She was going to regret this in the morning, especially if her little skit went viral. "All right," he said, stepping forward. "Tuck those phones away. The show is over."

A few grumbles later, the glow of the cell phones faded, and the crowd began to dissipate. Darryl turned back to Penelope, who sang, "You better watch out." At least if the clip went viral, she could carry a note.

"Penelope," he said, closing in on her, experiencing the same building heat he'd felt with her all those years ago.

She did a little twirl. "You better not pout." She pushed off one heel, wobbling slightly then quickly righted herself. "Something, something, something…gonna find out who's naughty or nice."

He chuckled. Christ, ten years ago, Penelope had been a mix of sexy and cute. That hadn't changed since he'd last seen her. He moved closer, not wanting the paperwork that came with an injury. Just like all those years ago, he couldn't take his eyes off her. He'd been as enthralled with her when she was a teenager. The night he'd given her that *hot* kiss, she'd worn tiny shorts and her exposed belly had been his entire focus. Even now, in her tight sweater and black leggings, she stirred things inside him that hadn't been stirred in a while.

The trouble with small towns, and being a cop, was Darryl knew *everyone,* and they knew that he and his ex-wife, Natalie, had divorced six months ago. Natalie had left town before the ink of the divorce papers had dried, and every well-meaning woman in town had been trying to help him "get over" his grief.

Now, Penelope had turned up, and he wondered if fate were giving him a chance to revisit his past. Unfortunately, it appeared that Penelope was in the habit of skirting the law. A law that Darryl had spent the past eight years enforcing. He'd put in his due and worked the night shifts since River Rock PD hired him. With a few cops retiring the next few months, there would be upcoming promotions, and the captain had already given Darryl the heads-up to bring his A game for the next while.

A promotion that he already fumbled once six months ago when Larry Michaels retired. The day Natalie had signed the divorce papers and left him, Darryl decided to spend the evening making friends with a bottle of whisky. He'd also made a complete ass out of himself at the local watering hole in town, Kinky Spurs. The next day, the promotion went to another cop.

That couldn't happen again.

Penelope sang another few lines, turning in a tight circle, and Darryl honestly doubted he could handle the likes of a grown-up Penelope Carter.

"Santa Claus—" Penelope screamed, as her heel caught on the edge of the fountain.

Darryl lurched forward when she began to fall. She landed with a yelp in his arms, and her wide green eyes connected with his. "All right?" he asked, ignoring the way her long, chocolate-colored hair felt damn soft against his hand.

Their gazes held for a beat. Then, she burst out laughing. A full-on belly laugh. One that Darryl never thought he'd ever experienced in his life.

"It's you," she finally said when she stopped laughing.

"It's me," he replied, ignoring the semi he was sporting from holding her so close. She smelled like sugar and vanilla, pure temptation.

"It's you," she repeated, snuggling her face into him like she belonged there. "Has anyone ever told you that you're warm and comfy, just like a big teddy bear?"

"I'm warm because it's freezing outside, and you're wearing only a sweater." He slowly placed her down, ensuring she was steady. When he let her go, he unzipped his coat and slid it over her shoulders. "And you are very drunk."

She giggled, her eyes bright. "I know. I think it was the forth." She held up her finger and hiccupped. "Nope, the fifth shot that did me in." She pulled his jacket around her, inhaling a big deep breath then grinning at him. "Seriously, you still smell so damn yummy. How is that even possible?"

Yeah, and he was rock hard now. Focusing away from what his little brain wanted, he turned to the laughing crowd who had obviously returned when Penelope fell. "I said the show was over, folks," he told them firmly. "Go home before anyone else gets in trouble."

"Oh, is that what I am...*in trouble*?"

Darryl's jaw clenched at the heat and promise in her voice before turning back to her. He found her heady gaze on him, lust burning through him. Or maybe it wasn't lust but the alcohol making her eyes glossy. "Come on, you little troublemaker. It's bedtime for you."

"Your bed, I hope." She grinned, pressing all those hot curves against him.

"Not tonight." *But maybe some night.* He shook the thought from his head, knowing this woman was not the type of woman for him to play around with. She'd likely be more of a headache than what it was worth. With his possible upcoming promotion, he could not have a smudge on his image, and this stunt was enough to tell him that he needed to stay clear of her. He took her gently by the arm and led her to the car, opening the door for her.

"So, you really a cop?" she asked, flopping into the passenger seat. "Can I see your handcuffs?"

"Yes, I am." He leaned down. "And no, you may not."

"Boo. How boring." She laughed.

Hyper aware of her in every regard, he reached for the seat belt then clipped her in.

"See, Mr. Police Officer, you like getting all close to me," she purred.

He turned his head after hearing the click, his mouth resting close enough to hers that all he needed to do was lean a little forward to claim those pouty lips. One little inch for him to find out if she still tasted as sweet as she smelled. "I don't recall having said that I didn't," he told her honestly.

His answer obviously surprised her, as her eyes widened ever so slightly. He grinned to himself, intrigued by the possibility he could surprise a woman like Penelope Carter. From what he learned from her cousins over the years, she'd been traveling and bartending her way along the coast. She'd seen it all, done it all, and experienced everything. But maybe one thing she hadn't seen was small-town life and a man like Darryl, who had promised himself to no longer keep quiet about what he wanted and be as honest and straightforward as possible. He'd compromised enough with his ex-wife, Natalie.

At Penelope's silence, he arched an eyebrow. Yeah, he'd play this game, and he'd play it better than her. "Nothing else to add, Ms. Carter?" he asked.

Her eyes rolled a little. "Ugh. I'm really drunk."

"I see that." He grabbed a plastic bag from this glove box and laid it out open on her lap. "If you're going to be sick, use the bag." He ensured her legs were all tucked in, his fingers tightening to linger there, and then he shut the door. He strode back to the driver's side door, a cloud of his breath leading the way, when suddenly the lights and siren flicked on, electrifying the dark night. "Trouble, yeah, sugar, that's you." He hurried into the car, flicking off the siren when he dropped into the seat, then he turned the ignition on and mumbled, "Can't seem to keep your hands to yourself, little menace. Police cars aren't toys." He turned to her. "Are you staying with your cousins?" His gaze hit those gorgeous legs again before moving up her body until he reached her face. She rested her head against the headrest, her face tilted toward him, her eyes shut. "Penelope." A beat. "Penelope."

She snored softly.

"It's not even a full moon," he grumbled and sighed. He reached over and gave her a little shake. "Penelope."

Nothing.

He stared at her then dropped his head back on his headrest, considering the best option now. He could call her cousins, the three Carter sisters who owned Three Chicks Brewery—a local craft brewery that was looking for its big break getting their locally famous beer, Foxy Diva distributed within North America—to find out where Penelope was staying. But somehow, that felt like the wrong move. The other choice was taking her to the station's drunk tank, but that wasn't quite right either.

"Let's just hope your trouble doesn't become *my* trouble," he told her before putting the car in drive.

CHAPTER TWO

EVERYTHING HURT WHEN Penelope woke the next morning. Her throat felt like sandpaper, her tongue lay dry in her mouth. Even her eyeballs burned. "Ugh. Bad shots. Bad, bad shots." It took an embarrassing amount of time for her to realize she wasn't in her bedroom at her cousins' house, but she was in a masculine bedroom with plain gray painted walls and big, dark wood furniture filling up the space. She slowly pushed up to sitting, taking a quick inventory of herself. Her sweater and leggings from last night were in place. Beside her, she found a glass of water and a note that read: *Drink Me.* Set next to the water were two painkillers and another note that read: *Don't Forget Us!* She did as instructed and downed both quickly, her head thumping like elephants were throwing a party inside of her skull.

The water hit her tongue first, a sweet relief, followed by her stomach clenching, reminding her that she was twenty-seven years old, not twenty-one, and shots were a terrible idea. Very, very *bad* idea. She returned the glass of water to the side table, when a low growl snapped her focus to the end of the bed.

There sat an orange cat that obviously ate more than he exercised. His brow was a tad darker than the rest of his face, giving him a scowl. "Hi, kitty," she said. "I'm a nice human. Promise."

The cat hissed, lurched forward, and swatted at her.

Penelope screamed, jumped on her pillows, trying to climb onto the headboard. The cat ended up directly in front of her, hissing and showing teeth. "Help," she screamed. "Help. It's going to kill me!"

Loud footsteps thundered up an obvious staircase and then drew closer. A beat later, the bedroom door whisked open. Penelope was momentarily stunned by *who* entered the bedroom: the manly six-foot-two, scruffy-bearded, dark brown-haired man that had stolen her heart when she was seventeen years old. The man who she compared every man to. The one that made it impossible to get serious with anyone because everyone else seemed flawed against Darryl Wilson.

When her gaze connected with his amber eyes, memories hit her in rapid succession. *Singing Christmas songs at the top of her lungs...skating on the fountain...sloppily flirting with him...* Dear God! Her cheeks burned, and suddenly the cat wasn't her biggest threat.

"Ebenezer, no!" Darryl snapped, charging into the room, scooping the cat up, who hissed, bit, then clawed his arm. "One sec," he said through gritted teeth before leaving the room.

In his place sat the cutest bloodhound, perched on the ground, his tongue wagging out the side of his mouth.

Penelope inhaled sharply as her lungs were desperate for air. On the end table, she noticed her cell phone and the little light beeping blue. She grabbed her phone, and slid down the headboard to land back onto the bed. Then she did what any sane woman would do—she hid under the duvet, hoping to God this was some terrible dream and soon she'd wake up.

Though when she unlocked her phone and saw the text message, she knew this morning was too messy to be anything else but *real* life. Messy was kinda her thing. In her dreams, she was so quiet and reserved, but in the real world, not so much.

Even though she knew the text message from the youngest Carter sister, Maisie, and would likely suck, she opened the message, hoping for the best. Then promptly cringed.

You better be dead. Okay, no, I hope you're not dead, but if you are alive, Clara is going to kill you. Please text. Everyone is worried about where you are.

"Shit," Penelope breathed, under her tent of peace that she never wanted to leave. She tried, like *really, really* tried not worry her family. Last night had definitely been a low point. Trying to fix her snafu, she texted back: I'm so sorry for worrying everyone. My phone died. Sometimes little lies helped fix truths that would only end in long discussions she didn't want to have. I'll be home soon. Promise. P.S. Tell Clara I'll bring her pie.

Pie fixed everything in the Carter household. Especially apple.

A creak of the floorboards, and Penelope froze.

"Not a very good hiding spot," Darryl said, amusement heavy in his low—*ridiculously seductive*—voice.

Penelope considered what he'd do if she didn't come out. Would he just leave? Then could she sneak out?

Dammit, he was a cop. He'd wait her out.

She slowly lowered the blanket, finding him leaning against the doorframe, arms folded across his wide chest and black T-shirt. Sweet Jesus. He looked even sexier this morning than when he was twenty years old. He belonged on a wilderness advertisement for some cologne that made women rip their panties off and throw them at him. And, like every elusive wilderness adventure hero, his expression was one hundred percent unreadable.

"Sorry about the cat," he said, eventually breaking the silence. "He's an asshole most days."

She snorted a laugh. "Really? He seemed so friendly."

The side of his sculpted lips, that she recalled seemed to be made for hot kisses, curved up. Damn. She was in so much trouble. She cleared her throat and dared to ask,

"What happened last night?"

One brow arched. "You don't remember?"

"I remember the singing and dancing, but after that, it's a blur."

He nodded, like he expected that answer. "I got you into my cruiser, and you passed out cold. I tried to wake you up, but that wasn't happening. So, it was either stay here at my place or the drunk tank at the station. What would you have preferred?"

"Here, so much *here*," she said, aware that she had to look like shit, and somehow feeling oddly self-conscious about that. A new thing for her. "Seriously, thank you so much." She paused, realizing something else too. "And thanks for not calling my cousins. I wouldn't have heard the end of that if I showed up at home in a cruiser."

"I suspected so." His mouth twitched. "Clara was in my graduating class."

Yeah, she figured Darryl probably knew her cousins even better than she did. She spent her childhood summers there in Colorado, for "fresh air" her parents said. But for the past ten years, she'd only talked over text and phone calls to her cousins.

Darryl wasn't moving, simply watching her. She stared into the strength of his eyes, feeling same flutter tickle in her belly that she felt when she'd met him at summer camp. An odd flutter, really. One she couldn't exactly understand, considering he also had that whole authoritative figure thing going on, which typically was a red flag for her.

Why was she even thinking about this?

She came to River Rock to be on her best behavior, and not to be the "wild child." Ready to get the hell out of Darryl's house and to fix her wrongs of last night with her cousins, she slid out of bed. "So...it's been a while, huh?"

"Ten years," he said.

"Wow, that long," she countered. Damn, now she was just being obvious that he rattled her a little. "Well, the ten years have been good to you." She quickly made the bed before turning back to him.

Heat flared in his eyes. "I'm not the only one."

Sweet Jesus. That voice. Those eyes. Darryl held a power that no man she'd met since him had. He made her belly flutter, heart race, and her regions south warm. And she had made a complete ass out of herself last night. "Thanks again for saving my butt last night, but I better get an Uber before my cousins kill me." She turned around and spotted her purse on the floor next to bed.

"Running away just like you did after I kissed you?"

She snatched her purse then slowly looked back at him, finding his hard stare on her. "I never stay in one place long," she told him. Not entirely true, but the reasons she left that night after their hot kiss at summer camp were so complicated, she didn't even know where to begin.

"Your cousins told me you've been traveling," he said flatly. Then he shook his head and added, "Never mind. It doesn't matter. Though…about you leaving. There might be a little problem with that."

In her hand, her phone beeped. She glanced at the screen. Maisie had texted back: Glad you're safe. Stay wherever you are. There's a wicked storm hitting us hard. I'll come get you once the roads are clear. Oh…and btw, where are you exactly?

Penelope blinked, processing that. "No, this cannot be happening." She rushed to the bedroom window and found a winter wonderland outside. "There's a storm?"

"A bad one," Darryl said, behind her. "We're going to have to ride this out. Unless you know of anyone with a snow mobile?"

"I don't know anyone here but my cousins, and I know they don't have one." Penelope glanced around, suddenly very aware that she stood in the bedroom of the guy who gave her a kiss she couldn't ever forget, and his bed was *right* there. "How long do we have to wait before the storm clears?" she asked, staying focused.

"Hmm…" Darryl sidled up next to her, and the masculine sandalwood scent of his cologne infused the air as he said, "By the looks of the clouds, I'd say we're in for another few inches of snow within the next couple hours."

Penelope pressed her face to the window and studied the sky. "You can seriously tell that?"

He chuckled.

She turned to him and frowned. "You're pulling my leg?"

"Just a little tug." He winked, leaning his shoulder against the wall, hand tucked into his pocket. "The weather station said we're likely to get hammered throughout the day and into the night. Hopefully the snow will stop in the early morning and then the plows can get the roads cleared."

She blinked. "Wait a second. Are you saying…?"

"That's right. You get another night with Ebenezer." He grinned before he turned away and left the bedroom. When he returned, he had a pair of tights and a T-shirt in his hands. "Thought you might want something a little more comfortable."

God, only then was Penelope reminded she still wore her clothes from last night. Clothes that suddenly made her feel dirty and disgusting. *Classy, Penelope. So friggin' classy!* But soon that thought faded away as she realized he'd handed her another woman's clothing. *His ex-wife's?* Maisie told Penelope when Darryl married after college, and she also told her when he divorced six months ago. Penelope eyed the clothing in her hands.

Darryl gave another low laugh. "They're my sister

Ashley's clothes," he explained gently. "She lives in England right now with her boyfriend but stays here when she visits and always forgets some of her stuff." His gaze traveled her body all the way to Penelope's toes and then back up to her face. "You look about the same size."

"Gotcha. Okay, thanks," Penelope said, cursing her now puckering nipples.

He gestured at the hallway with a flick of his chin. "The bathroom is the second door on the right. Take a shower, a bath, whatever you want. I'll make us breakfast."

Penelope nodded, staring into the warmth of his eyes. Most men Penelope could read easily. They were always looking for one thing—which, usually, she was too—but *this* guy didn't seem like someone who would stop once his own itch was scratched. Darryl seemed like the type who took his time with a woman because he cared that she left his bed satisfied.

Not why you're here!

He slowly arched an eyebrow. "Problem?"

"Nope, not a single one," she said, and strode past him.

One night. Then she'd be outta there. Easy-peasy.

THE UPSTAIRS WATER running through the pipes turned

off, and Darryl placed another log into the wood-burning fireplace in his small living room of his 18th century home. His mother, as a single parent, had purchased the property back when Darryl was five years old, and he'd lived in the house ever since. Minus the time he'd spent in Denver for college then police academy, but with all its little quirks like creaky floorboards and loud pipes, this was home. The three-bedroom house wasn't impressive by any means, but it had good bones and old-fashioned charm with thick baseboards, a large stone fireplace mantel, and even gingerbread trim along the wrap-around front porch.

The firewood crackled and popped when a sudden creak came behind him. Damn, his sister and her tight clothes. The T-shirt hugged Penelope's body, accentuating every luscious curve, drawing his full attention. Her hair was damp around her makeup-free face. She momentarily stunned him. He'd thought she'd grown into a beautiful woman before, but all natural seemed ever better. Fresher. Realer, somehow. "How do you take your coffee?" he asked, moving toward the kitchen off to the right of the living room.

"Cream only," she answered behind him.

He stepped into the small eat-in kitchen with the round oak table that hadn't changed since Darryl was a kid. After taking a mug off the bamboo countertop, he hurried to make her coffee how she liked it. On his way into the living room again, he grabbed the plate with a blueberry muffin and cut-up fruit. He found her on the brown leather couch in front of the fire, with the fuzzy blanket his sister bought him one year for Christmas settled over her lap. Her gaze, disappointingly, was not on him; it was on Ebenezer, who death-stared at her from the chair across from her.

"He'll only bite if you sit on his chair," Darryl said, handing her the mug and plate.

She lifted a single eyebrow at him. "He can have that chair, and the rest of the house for that matter. Is he always so mean?"

"Yup, he was that way when we found him."

She watched Ebenezer while she sipped her coffee then lifted her mug at Darryl after her sip. "Thanks for breakfast, by the way."

Darryl smiled. "Quite welcome."

She placed her coffee mug down on the table then unwrapped the muffin. "Not to be rude or anything, but can I ask *why* you got a cat like him?" She gave Ebenezer a quick look then lowered her voice like the cat could understand her. "I mean, he's cute in a feral cat kinda way, but seriously, what's got him so pissed off?"

Darryl grabbed his mug and his plate from the coffee table he'd set down earlier, then dropped beside her. "I had no part in bringing Ebenezer into this family. That was all Tyson."

"Who's Tyson?" She bit into the muffin.

"Penelope, meet Tyson." He gestured to the big lazy bloodhound lying in front of the fireplace, sprawled out like he was sun tanning. "He's the station's search-and-rescue dog, but don't be fooled, he owns me."

She smiled and then chewed a bit before asking, "Okay, so how did Tyson find Ebenezer?"

Darryl finished his sip of coffee, returning his mug to the table. "Ty sniffed him out behind a dumpster." The day after Natalie left their marriage to go home to Wisconsin to be with her family. "He was in bad shape, so I brought him back here, and Ty and I nursed him back to health."

"Okay, seriously nice of you, but"—Penelope frowned at the cat—"I actually think he wants to kill me."

"It's not just you," Darryl reassured her. "It's everyone."

"Even you?" she asked with wide eyes.

To prove his point, Darryl rose, still holding onto his plate, and got close to the cat. Ebenezer's hair stood straight up, and he hissed like a rabid animal. "He hates me as much as he hates anyone. The only one he tolerates is Ty. Sometimes I see them sleeping together when they think I'm not looking." Darryl returned to his seat next to her. "But to be honest, I think he's just cold and uses Ty for warmth."

Penelope studied the cat who began licking his paw, with his glare still set on her. "Not to sound insensitive or anything, but why do you keep a cat who hates you?"

Darryl barked a laugh, leaning back against the couch. "You say that like I have some authority over him. He is the owner of this house. Don't let yourself believe anything different."

She smiled softly then frowned at the cat. "Is he scowling at me?"

"Yup," Darryl confirmed, taking a bite of his muffin.

"Okay, so that's weird." She turned her attention to her breakfast. They ate in silence, and Darryl took the opportunity to eat his two muffins and half a plate of fruit before she said, "I guess I should probably thank you for taking care of me last night."

He glanced sideways, examining her piercing eyes. "You always get three sheets to the wind?"

She held his gaze firmly. "Why did you and your wife break up?"

His mouth twitched at her deflection. Yeah, she was setting him straight well enough—it'd been ten years and he had no business asking anything personal. But he had nothing to hide, not a damn thing. "Natalie and I began dating the fall after you and I shared that intense kiss." He liked the way her cheeks heated at the reminder that no, he had not forgotten how sweet she tasted that night. "We married about a year after college. By the time our twenty-fifth birthdays rolled around, we were two different people. By our twenty-seventh birthdays, we had become two of the very best friends. By twenty-nine, Natalie fell in love with someone else, and by thirty, we were divorced."

Penelope shut her parted lips, then eventually said, "Wow. Look at you just putting everything out there like that."

"It is what it is," he replied with a shrug. "Besides, I'm surprised you already don't know everything about everyone. This town is full of gossipers, and I have no doubt your cousins are among them."

She regarded him intently as she took another nibble of her muffin. "Well, of course, I knew you were divorced, but Maisie didn't say what happened." She rubbed her fingers together over the plate, dusting off the muffin crumbs, then she gave a small shrug. "I guess fair is fair. To answer your question, no, I don't always drink like that, but me and Christmas have problems."

"What kind of problems?"

"The music, the endless joy shoved down your throat, the angry shoppers. All of it."

At that, he cracked a smile. "You were the one singing Christmas carols last night."

She winced. "Yeah, let's pretend that didn't happen."

His smile widened. "Not sure you'll be able to forget that. And neither will the people who videoed you on their cell phones."

"Great." She let out a long heavy sigh, dropping her head back onto the couch. "Video evidence is the worst kind of evidence."

"Not in my line of work, it's not."

She gave a little nod of agreement.

He became curious. "So, you got drunk to survive Christmas?"

She nodded and gave a cute smile. "And apparently, I also skated on fountains in high heels."

"It was impressive, I gotta say."

"More like embarrassing." She hid her face in her hands and muttered something incoherent before saying clearly, "I'm never going to hear the end of it once Clara finds out." She lowered her hands and gave him a tight look. "I mean, Amelia will probably just smooth things over like she does, and Maisie will laugh then try and support me, but Clara is going to murder me." She raised her fingers and did quotations marks. "'Penelope, we have a reputation in River Rock. Don't mess that up.'"

"That's Clara, I take it?"

Penelope nodded and her eyes cast downward.

"Ah, it wasn't so bad," he said, trying to reassure her. He'd seen people do far more embarrassing things when they were drunk, including naked things. "Well, maybe your singing was pretty terrible, but you can live that down."

"Hey!" She picked up a throw pillow next to her and tossed it at him. "My singing is just fine, thank you very much."

Good, he had her laughing. Her singing was actually great.

She took another nibble of her muffin, staring into the fire, while Ty snored loudly, before she addressed him again. "How about you? Is Christmas a big thing for you?" she asked.

He shrugged. "I'm a cop; we do a lot for the community throughout the holidays." Then something more important occurred to him. "Why aren't you with your family this Christmas?"

She tossed the last piece of muffin into her mouth. "No one wanted me there."

He stilled, looking for any hint of hurt in her expression. He found none. "What do you mean, no one wanted you?"

She stared blankly at the flickering flames. "My mom told me she thought it was best that I didn't come home for Christmas this year. My dad said he was traveling, even though I know he isn't." She turned to face him again, and her honest soft smile indicated to him that being hurt by her parents was a regular occurrence. "They divorced that year I met you. That's why they pulled me out of camp to come home."

Damn, he'd wondered so many times why she'd left

so abruptly. He wondered if he'd come on too strong. Now he had his answer. And he almost wished the real reason was because he'd scared her off.

She pulled her legs up, leaning a little on her side to face him better. "When I was younger, my dad flew me in to stay with Auntie Rose to get me away from the fighting for the summers, I guess. I got the job at the summer camp just for fun and something to do. But that summer, my mom dragged me out to prove to my dad she had won. By eighteen, I was done with the fighting and being used as a pawn in their divorce. Besides, they both had new families and new kids, and I don't really fit into the mold of their new lives."

He didn't like what he was hearing. And suddenly, he began to wonder what going through that experience would do to a woman's heart? "So that's why you came back here after all this time away?"

She nodded. "Maisie demanded I come when she heard I'd be spending Christmas alone."

He liked Maisie Carter. She was a little bit like Penelope, a free spirit, only slightly less *free,* since she didn't get the police called on her for skating on a fountain. "You're close, you two?"

"We were the best of friends when they lived in California." She tossed a grape into her mouth. "It was kinda heartbreaking when the family picked up and moved here after their grandfather got sick. But that's why my parents sent me out here for the summers. I loved it here."

He watched the fire a moment, still coming to grips that it hadn't been his fault she'd left after he kissed her. He'd thought for years that it had been because he'd told her he wanted to kiss her forever. He still couldn't believe he told her that. He took a long sip of his coffee to gather his thoughts and then turned back to her. "Where does your family live now?"

"My mom still lives in Cali, and my dad moved to Portland. When they divorced, I think they both wanted to rediscover themselves, so I moved out and traveled across the US working odd jobs, until I could bartend, then I worked in everything from pubs, to resorts, to dive bars, to tourist traps, and even some night clubs along the coast." She paused to shrug again. "My parents' new families are just...*different.* I don't fit in."

"You're strong and a free spirt," Darryl stated, some-how feeling the need to point out what assholes her parents were. "That can intimidate people."

She grinned, leaning forward, staring at him deeply. "Does that mean I can intimidate a big, bad cop like you?"

Christ, the heat she brought in a single second blew his mind apart. One second, *nothing.* The next, her whole being seemed to light up with desire. In that regard, Penelope hadn't changed one bit. She still made him hungry very easily. He had to fight the pull of his body to lean forward and find out what would happen if he played with that heat a little. "You could try." He grinned some of the *need* back at her.

Her lips parted in an invitation, and it took all of his strength not to claim the kiss she was offering him. She was trouble. That he knew for a fact. He needed to be squeaky clean until Christmas was over, since everyone in the department was looking at him for his possible promotion. But his promotion wasn't here in his house with them right now; all the worries he thought of before now were gone. It was just him and her, and he was slowly beginning to think she might be the right kind of trouble.

CHAPTER THREE

T HE NIGHT CREPT up fast, and Penelope almost
regretted that. She'd enjoyed the day with Darryl,
far more than she originally thought she would this
morning, considering she was hungover and embarrassed
to her bones. Darryl had a lot of stories, funny ones, and
they'd watched two movies and talked throughout both.
She guessed this was what people did during the
holidays. Relaxed, spent time with friends and family,
and stayed cozy inside by the fire. She hadn't spent a day
like this with anyone for a really long time. Most of the
time, she worked all night long and slept through the
daylight hours or traveled. And after her low-key day
with Darryl, she wasn't exactly sure how she felt about
that. Had she been missing out on life?

They had sandwiches for lunch and played a game of
cards. Then they'd made lasagna for dinner, and she'd
been washing dishes when Darryl's back porch caught
her eye. He'd ventured off to the washroom, and when
she finished the dishes, she hurried out the door,
grabbing the warm blanket on her way. She slipped into

Darryl's big winter boots, and like some kid, she dragged her feet through the snow until she stood in middle of his backyard.

She wrapped the blanket around her shoulders tight to keep out the brisk air and tipped her head back, opening her mouth and letting big snowflakes fall on her tongue. The light from the porch spilled out, and the night was quiet and peaceful. There wasn't a speck of green or brown anywhere. White coated the world; a cold, bitter night that was somehow the most beautiful thing she'd seen in a while.

"Here."

She glanced next to her, finding Darryl offering her a mug of hot chocolate.

"You keep little marshmallows in your house?" she asked him.

He shook his head with a dry laugh. "I have these hot chocolate packages for a Christmas event that's coming up. Figured you might like one."

She took a tiny sip of the piping hot chocolate, steaming up in the cold air. "I do, thank you." She turned back to the evergreen trees around his yard, with its branches dropping from the heavy snow. "It's so beautiful out here."

"It's also freezing," he said, zipping up his coat.

"But pretty too," she countered, unable to look away at the glistening snow. "I've been traveling around so much that I think I forgot how pretty the snow really is."

"You don't have a home base?"

Penelope glanced sideways at him, finding his gaze soft. She shook her head. "I haven't for a really long time. I get antsy whenever I stay somewhere too long. I like the wind in my hair and the adventure that awaits me."

"Sounds like a fun way to live."

"It is." But even as she said that, it seemed like a half-truth. At one time in her life, she loved picking up and going anywhere. She lived for the adventure. Now, she wondered if there would ever be a place that would make her stick. "Did you join the force right after college?" she asked before taking another sip from her mug.

He shoved his hands into his pockets. "Yup."

"Kinda one of those always-knew-what-you-wanted-to-be types of things."

He nodded. "My father was a lowlife. I didn't want to be like him, so I made sure I was the exact opposite."

She'd never known anyone who escaped a bad situation just to prove he could. This guy was born from some other material than all the people she'd ever met before. "You are a strange breed of human," she told him.

His brows furrowed. "In what way?"

"You have all sorts of integrity, and you share personal shit really easily."

He shrugged. "Yeah, that was one of the good things to happen from my divorce. I don't keep stuff inside so much. It is what it is. You asked. I answered."

"That's probably the cop in you, you know, all honest and brave," she said with a soft laugh.

"Probably." He winked.

She drew in a long, deep breath, embracing the cold air sliding through her lungs. "Most people I meet are like me."

"Wild?" he offered.

She laughed. "A little untamed, sure."

He rocked back on his heels. "Well, this Christmas, let's hope skating on a fountain is as wild as you get, sugar."

An odd sense of warmth slid through her that had nothing to do with the hot cup of hot chocolate she held. "*Sugar,* that's a new one. You call every girl that?"

"Just you." He winced, a blush tinging his cheek.

Interesting. She paused to cock her head. "Just me, huh? Why is that?"

A slow shiver slid over her when he leaned in close and inhaled deeply, his eyes fluttering shut. "You smell like my mother's Christmas sugar cookies." His eyes reopened, and he gave her a look so warm that on his tough exterior, it seemed surprising. "It's a smell that brings back good memories for me."

A little rattled by his nearness, and his truth, she

cleared her throat. "Your mom doesn't bake cookies anymore?"

He shook his head, glancing at the trees now. "My mom passed away a few years back from a heart attack."

His expression was closed off, a mask of strength for sure, and yet there was something tender there, too. "God, that's awful, Darryl. I'm sorry. Maisie never told me."

"I was really sorry for a long time too." He turned to her, the light from the porch highlighting the hard masculine lines of his jaw. "Christmas is a hard time for my sister, Ashley, because our mom died on Christmas Eve."

Penelope didn't know what to say, so she gently asked, "Are you close with your sister?"

"Very close. She calls every few days and texts the days she doesn't call."

"Lucky you," Penelope said, letting a little honesty out herself. "I always wanted a sister. Well, like a real sister, not a stepsister I never see who thinks I'm her nemesis."

He smiled. "Life's a bitch like that, really. You never do get the shit you want, do you?"

"Sure, you do," she countered. "You just have to go and grab what you want by the balls until it's yours."

The strands of his hair covered in fallen snow fell over his brow. "Is that what you do in life, Penelope?

Grab things by the balls?"

She shrugged. "I mean, you could go with the whole 'lick it' and then it becomes yours, if you like."

"Now *that* I can get on board with."

The heat in his voice made the chill in the air all but vanish, and instinctually she found herself turning to him, just like she had at summer camp. For those five days, he had been the guy she couldn't stop looking at, flirting with, giggling over. But she wasn't a kid anymore, and neither was he. Darryl's gaze was on hers, all warmth and strength. Things she simply was not used to. She dated surfers, wild adventurers like herself. Not a small-town cop who lived life on the straight and narrow, and never left home. Especially a cop who had taken her in because she'd been a drunken idiot last night.

And yet…*and yet,* there was a pull there. An impulse for her to jump on *this* adventure. She'd never been the type who didn't listen to that voice in her head, and she wasn't about to stop now. That voice had led her up and down the West Coast and had given her unforgettable memories. That voice allowed her to find a place in this world when she didn't seem to fit in anywhere. That voice had led her to River Rock this Christmas.

"Penelope," Darryl said softly, almost a warning.

She stepped closer until she was pressed against him, noting that he did not step away. "Yes, Darryl?"

"This might not be the best idea," he said, taking his

hands from his pockets and sliding one along the small of her back, pulling her in nice and close, even as his voice rang with hesitation.

"You're single, aren't you?"

"I am."

She could feel his resistance in the tightness of his shoulders. Yet there was only heat, desire, and need in his smoldering gaze. "I leave after Christmas day for a job on a cruise ship." That was the next adventure, cruising along the Caribbean, bartending on the open seas. She pressed herself against the hardest part of him. "I can feel that you want me in a big, bad way, so what's the hold up?"

He stared down at her, gaze flaring. Hard. His jaw muscles working overtime.

"I get it," she added when silence greeted her. "You're the good guy. The one who does the right thing, all the time. But here's the thing: I'm not the good girl. I'm the *fun* girl. And this girl wants this good guy in hot, *hot* ways. So, let's make a deal. We've got tonight, then if fate intervenes again, we'll have a few more nights. I hate Christmas, and what would make this Christmas better is a whole lot of sex with *you*."

Darryl's head tilted just a little as his heated gaze fell to her lips. A wild shiver danced from her fingers to her toes when everything changed about him, all the clean-cut, upstanding citizen stuff was gone. Here stood a *man* who wanted and needed things that were not going to put him on the nice list. "You. Are. Trouble," he said, dropping his mouth closer to hers.

She stood on her tiptoes and placed her hands his square chest, feeling the hard thumps of his heartbeat. "I know you don't know this, yet, but that's what makes me fun."

FROZEN SOLID, NOT only from the icy air, but from Penelope's lips sliding against his, Darryl moaned, pulled under by her spell. A spell that most people wouldn't understand because Penelope didn't seem to be his type from the outside. Sure, she was beautiful, but her personality seemed to be at complete odds with his. In fact, he had no doubt, even as his tongue danced with hers and his lips moved over hers, that somewhere along the way, she'd cause him—hopefully only mildly painful—aggravation.

Yet when she leaned away and asked, "All right?" he knew right then, there was no chance he'd walk away from her.

He took the mug from her hand and tossed it into the snow drift next to him. "Yeah, I'm all right, sugar." He needed her heat again. Years had gone by since he felt anything remotely close to what Penelope made him feel with one kiss. *Want.*

She planted another kiss on him, harder this time, offering a little bit more. And he took all she had to give him, putting aside that she could become a complication. Fate had brought her back into his life, and he needed to *feel* this with her. Plus, her taste, her smell…he threaded his fingers into her hair, tilted her head and deepened the kiss, taking it where he wanted it to go. To a much dirtier place. She moaned, and that sound sent his muscles flexing. He gathered her in his arms, and she wrapped her legs tight around his waist as he led them back inside. He kicked the door shut behind them, and he caught a quick flash of beautiful hooded eyes before he pulled the blanket off her shoulders and pressed her back against the wall in his kitchen. He kissed her deeper now, letting out the intensity he felt the night he'd given her that first hot kiss.

Passion, desire, it'd all felt dead inside him for so long. *This* woman brought that back. And Darryl wasn't thinking repercussions when he carried her up the staircase and entered his bedroom. Nor did he think what may happen after this, when he lay her out on the mattress. He reached for his coat and shrugged out of that before taking his shirt over his head and tossing it aside before lowering his body onto hers.

She arched up into him, grinding the junction be-tween her thighs against his hardened length. Her hands explored him, her fingers sliding across every groove of muscle along his chest and stomach, and he shut his eyes, reveling in how good *touch* felt. Her lips returned to his, and she gave all of herself in her kiss. And he demanded even more after that, threading his fingers into her hair, thrusting his tongue deeper into her mouth, urged on by her sexy moans.

When need drove him wild, he ground his throbbing cock against her, circling his hips, and felt the heat of her, the need. He reached for her T-shirt, removing that until she lay in her bra. He flicked the hooks free, then he kissed his way along her shoulders where he slid off her bra. He open-mouth kissed along her collarbone then to her breasts where he took one in his hand and squeezed until he sucked a nipple, and she arched into the pleasure.

Paying attention there, he teased her taut buds, sucking, biting, swirling, until her hands came into his hair, pinning him there. He groaned, his balls aching when her hands slid between their and she began shoving off his pants. When she had those and his boxer briefs down below his ass, a hot tremor ran through him as her hand wrapped around his cock and stroked him. He bit her nipple lightly and she shivered, giving a moan for more. Damn. He'd give her whatever she wanted...anything she wanted, as long as she didn't stop stroking him. Her hand squeezed tight, circling the tip and running down his shaft.

Blinded by the pleasure, he reached between them, sliding his fingers over her yoga pants, feeling her dampness through the thin fabric. "So wet, Penelope. You want me." He squeezed her sex, then gently tickled his fingers across her sensitive flesh until he had her squirming, wanting his touch so badly that she angled her hips up, begging him for it.

"Yes." She gasped. "Darryl!"

"Ah, but what if I like you like this?" he asked her. "Seeing you out of your mind?"

Her nails dug into his arms and her chin titled back. "Darryl, I'm about to come already." A little fact about Penelope Carter occurred to him, then. She may be wild, but not with her body. Either she'd been longing for him, or she hadn't been with anyone in a while.

Heat spiraled to his groin, making him desperate to bring them both something good this Christmas. One night. That's what they had. He planned to take his fill. He lifted his hips a little, placing his weight on one arm. "Is this where you want me?" he asked, stroking her warm sex.

"Yes." She gasped again, chin pointing up now.

Rich masculine satisfaction flooded him. A sensation that seemed so foreign until it returned now. He slipped his hand inside her yoga tights, instantly connecting with her wet, shaved pussy. He stroked her hard clit, pressing and circling the bud until she was barely kissing him anymore, her mouth open with her moans. That's when he slipped one finger inside her heat, then another.

Her body shook. "Jesus. I'm…."

"Going to break apart for me." He thrust harder and faster, until her body stiffened. Until her moans became loud. He didn't stop thrusting his fingers until she arched off the bed, her toes pointing out, and she shuddered and screamed her pleasure.

He smiled, all for himself, and squeezed her sex with each hard tremor she gave. Damn, he still had it. Something he'd wondered for a long time.

When her quivering stopped and her body relaxed, he slowly removed his hand from her pants, and she eventually opened her eyes and gave him a smile, promising delicious sex. She wiggled out from under him, and with her beautiful round breasts all for his viewing pleasure, she shimmied out of her yoga tights. "Condom?" she asked, breathless.

He opened the drawer to the box of unopened condoms he'd bought a few weeks ago, thinking he'd try to scratch an itch over the holidays, not even realizing Penelope Carter would be barreling into his life for Christmas. She grabbed one, then kept her pretty eyes on him when she climbed onto his lap like she'd been there a thousand times before. Confident and sexy as hell, she straddled his thighs then took his cock in her hands and began stroking him. He pushed up on his arms, watching her as she dragged his pre-cum over the tip and slid it down his shaft, somehow making him even harder.

She gave him a sexy smile. "You're fun to play with."

"You're damn good at playing."

That smile only burned hotter as she stroked him. He had never recalled a day in his life when a hand job did anything for him but finish the job when he needed to finish. She stared right at him and then dropped some saliva onto his cock to stroke him again. The pleasure was enough to make him damn near cross-eyed. And when that pleasure began to steal his control, he shifted to gather her in his arms.

She pressed against his chest. "You stay right there."

He arched an eyebrow. "Is that how we're playing this?"

"Yes, Mr. Officer." She grinned, ripping open the wrapper, and sheathed him, slowly dragging the latex over his stretched skin. When she climbed farther up his body, she kissed his stomach, then his chest, and he wasn't even sure he was breathing anymore. She slid her mouth over his neck, and then she lowered onto him in the same second, taking him deep inside her as she whispered, "God, you feel so amazing."

He grunted his answer, dropping his hands onto her hips as she slowly worked herself over him. Up and down, she rode him, her hands coming to his face as she kissed him. The woman knew what she was doing, and his mind began to fade as she moved away from his mouth to sit straighter and began thrusting her hips back and forth until she was grinding against him.

Fuck. She was *sexy*.

Her tits were bouncing. Her hips moving fast, claiming her pleasure, and damn, did she claim his too.

She dropped her head, her long hair tickling his chest as she worked her hips, harder and faster. He gripped her waist, helping her gain speed, feeling her inner muscles squeezing at him, telling him she was going to get there.

He needed her to get there. Because he was getting there too. His cock ached to blow with every perfect squeeze of her sweet pussy. She looked too good. She smelled too good. She felt so fucking incredible. His eyes pinched shut and heat roared up his spine when she fell into her climax, writhing atop him. He roared his pleasure, lifting her hips, and pumped into her from underneath.

The world faded away except for the darkness and the strain of his body, until the pulsating pleasure washed over him.

Sometime later, in the darkness of his bedroom, Penelope's soft voice pulled him back to her. "I have a strange admission to make," she said, breathless.

She lay atop him, dead weight, her soft breasts pressing against his rising and falling chest. He slid his hand up her damp back. "What's that?"

She lifted up to look him in the eye, looking messy and perfect all at the same time. "I don't regret for one second that you found me last night skating on the fountain in my high heels."

He chuckled and kissed her. "Neither do I."

CHAPTER FOUR

*W*AS A DRIVE *of shame worse than a walk of shame?*

Penelope contemplated that very thought on the drive to her cousins' house the following morning, with a fresh baked apple pie resting on her lap that they'd grabbed on the drive over. The aroma of sugar and cinnamon filled Darryl's cruiser, as the warmth rested against her thighs. Snow drifts hugged the road and the sun glistened off the bright white snow as far as the eye could see. Darryl sat next to her, playing the part of hot cop in his uniform with his dark navy-blue winter coat, one hand slung over the top of the steering wheel, taking the roads slow and easy. Tyson slept on the back seat, sprawled out like the holidays had already begun, and he'd eaten far too much. And Ebenezer stayed out of her way after their first introduction but scowled all the same on her way out the door.

All in all, her body was tender in all the right places, her chest lighter than it had been in months. And fate had given her Darryl back for a little longer to finish the fantasy that had begun with that one hot kiss by the lake.

Maybe Christmas wasn't going to be so bad after all.

Darryl pulled his cruiser into the long driveway, hugged by evergreens that painted a pretty snowy picture this morning, and Penelope decided any type of shame didn't leave her in the best light. The driveway ended at a big, white, colonial-style house with the black barn now turned into a brewery off to the right. Cars lined the small parking lot off to the left, not really a surprise being Saturday morning. Three Chicks Brewery was part of the brewery tour put on by local tour companies for vacationers. The middle Carter sister, Amelia, was heading into the barn with the morning tour, wearing jeans and fluffy boots.

Right as Darryl pulled his cruiser to a stop, his cell phone rang, and he grabbed it from the cup holder. "Wilson," he answered. A pause. "Yes, sir." A pause then his gaze flicked to Penelope. "Yeah, I've got an idea on that." Another pause. "Shouldn't be a problem." Another pause. "Thank you, sir."

When Darryl ended the call, Penelope had a bad feeling "That call was about me, wasn't it?" she asked.

Darryl placed his cell back into the cup holder. "Yup, and you're going to be my elf."

She paused, waiting for him to correct himself. When he didn't, she guffawed. "I'm going to be your *what*?"

"My elf," he repeated easily with a sexy smile that

made her belly flip-flop. "That was my captain. The video of your late-night skating has been uploaded to YouTube, so apparently, I need to handle this matter."

She felt the widening of her eyes. "And how does one exactly handle me?"

He leaned forward a little, deepened his voice, and his tone turned sultry. "Now, Penelope, I would think by the three times last night and twice this morning, you would know exactly how I handle you."

Damn, her nipples tightened. Breath hitched. Lower half warmed and dampened. Yeah, apparently her body was well aware of all Darryl could do. "That's not what I meant," she said anyway. "What exactly did your captain mean?"

Darryl winked and then his expression slid back into that of *hard cop.* "It means I need to show those watching—"

"Which is who?" she interjected, knowing she wasn't going to like what he said next.

"The mayor, the captain, my fellow cops," he explained, "that I'm not letting you off with a slap on the hand. That your little skating escapade is not one this town will tolerate from drunk tourists. The last thing we need is for that fountain to become some sort of social media booze challenge."

Penelope decided she was not a fan of the the strait-laced side of Darryl. "Seriously?"

"Seriously."

Terrible things filled her mind. She finally decided the reality couldn't be worse than getting slapped with an expensive fine she couldn't afford. "All right, so what's my punishment? It's not a fine, is it?"

"There is that possibility." He cocked his head, examining her. "But that hardly seems very Christmas-y, does it?"

"Nope, not Christmas-y at all," she said in relief. She was barely able to pay her bills, living paycheck to paycheck. During the high tourist season, she was rolling in cash, but all the traveling and relocating and finding new places to crash for a few weeks or months made all her money bleed out.

He gave her a long look then settled into his seat. "Here's where we're at: It's either a thousand-dollar fine and possible 180 days in jail for drunk and disorderly." She died a little, and by the slight amusement glistening in his eyes, he knew it. "Or you're going to be my helper elf during the police station events over the holidays, ending with a barn dance on Christmas Eve."

"But I leave the day after Christmas," she reminded him. "Being your elf will take up all my free time before I go."

He grinned back. "But you'll leave with a clear record."

She pondered her next steps. There wasn't a way out

of this. Besides, maybe spending more time with Darryl wasn't such a bad thing. That could lead to more sex. Right? "Okay, so what's the plan, then?"

"I'll pick you up tomorrow morning at nine o'clock."

"Perfect," she said with a bite of sarcasm. "I'll go find my Christmas spirit and see you tomorrow."

She went to move away when he grabbed her chin, and somehow, that hold made her freeze. She stared into his eyes, lost in them. She was flighty. He was not. And that tight hold made her body awaken just like that, almost as if he could ground her. Darryl was this big, warm spot that she wanted to mold into. Hang on to, even. More than anything, every time he touched her, she felt like that teenage girl who didn't know the dark ways life could be. She wanted to be that girl again.

"I enjoyed last night." His lips twitched. "And this morning." Then his mouth dropped to hers, and she forgot she was in his cruiser. It became only about the way she felt when his lips glided against hers. How in this second, they got their moment back, and they were taking it.

When he broke the kiss, she smiled, attempting to hide the heat he brought. Needing to get away, considering she was tempted to rip that uniform off him to get to all those hard muscles underneath, and to get his hands on her again because those hands knew what they were doing and then some, she opened the car door and hurried out. "I'll see you tomorrow, then," she said, leaning her head back into the cruiser.

"You will." He grinned.

The last thing she saw was his captivating eyes promising so many hot things. Then she shut the door, carefully holding the apple pie. She trotted up the front porch, the old wood creaking under her high heels.

Before she could even reach for her keys, the dark cherry-painted front door opened. Clara, the oldest Carter sister, stood in the doorway. Her reddish brown hair was pulled into a tight ponytail. She wore skinny jeans and a long sweater, covering her legs that went on and on. Her deep blue eyes were narrowed, a frown on her oval face. "You seduced the local law enforcement?"

"What's seduced, Mommy?"

Clara's eyes widened before she spun around, staring at her six-year-old son, Mason. He was cute as a button, with huge light green eyes and light brown hair. Both of those traits belonged to Mason's father, who had always been a mystery. Clara never said who Mason's father was, only that he wasn't in their lives and didn't want to be.

As cool and calm as she always was, Clara took the pie from Penelope then handed it to Mason. "Here, honey, take this into the kitchen for Mommy. Don't drop it."

Mason yanked the pie away then ran into the kitchen. A bang and some shuffling of feet, and Clara shook her head. "He totally dropped it." She sighed, glancing back at Penelope, her frown sliding back into place. "You promised you'd be good."

"I was good." She smiled, shutting the door behind her. "Very good, in fact." And so was Darryl. *In bed.* God, he was so good; she still tingled in all the places he'd touched. Maybe it was their history. Her longing for the guy who gave her that *hot* kiss, the guy who made her heart sing by saying he wanted to kiss her like that every day. That man had gifts and he knew how to use them.

Footsteps thundered along the hallway, then Maisie appeared on the top of the staircase. Her dirty blond hair was swept into a side braid, her pink Converse moved quick as she hurried down the staircase, her dark round blue eyes locked onto Penelope. "Oh, my God, tell me *everything.*"

"There's nothing to tell."

"Liar." Maisie pointed to Penelope's face. "I saw Darryl kissing you in his cruiser. That's a kiss from a man who got some."

"I need more coffee for this conversation," Penelope said, moving into the small farmhouse kitchen with the old worn white cabinets and black countertop. She grabbed a mug and made herself another coffee. The one at Darryl's house wasn't going to cut it today.

"Mason?" Clara called, entering the kitchen.

The pie box was on the kitchen island, slightly lopsided. The boy was nowhere in sight.

"Ooh, pie," Maisie said, sidling up next to Penelope. She opened the box. "Messy pie, but still pie."

When Maisie went for the plates, Penelope took a sip of her coffee. Clara always added cinnamon into the coffee before it brewed, and Penelope hugged the mug at the nutmeggy taste.

Amelia strode into the kitchen, then. All three Carter sisters shared the same slender body shape, but where they differed was in their hair, and Amelia's had long ginger colored hair, which was a pretty contrast to her bright blue eyes. She took one look at Clara then at the pie, then smiled at Penelope. "Wondered when you'd find your way back to us." She stepped closer and made herself a coffee, then whispered, "Saw you on YouTube. You were hilarious."

"Don't tell Clara," Penelope begged.

"I won't. Promise." Amelia lifted the mug to her lips, and before she drank, she said, "I like you alive."

Penelope cringed, but Maisie thrust a plate at her. She accepted it with a smile then dropped down onto a stool at the kitchen island. "Anything exciting happen while I've been trapped in the snowstorm?"

"Oh, no, you don't," Clara said, moving closer, ignoring the pie, and folding her arms. "You promised you weren't going to be any trouble."

"I'm not being any trouble," Penelope countered. "In

fact, I've decided to help Darryl over the holidays with some of the Christmas events the police are putting on."

Amelia's shoulders shook with her laughter. Okay, so she obviously suspected this wasn't exactly a voluntary venture.

"Really?" Clara said, some of her scowl lessening. "When did this happen?"

"Just a few minutes ago," Penelope explained, cutting into her pie with her fork then devouring a big bite.

"Hmm," Clara said. "Well then, I'm sorry I misjudged you. We just have a lot riding on our reputations right now."

They did, Penelope knew that. The three sisters had inherited the property when their grandfather passed away. Instead of selling it, they all sold their houses and apartments and moved into the brewery, giving up their jobs to take their grandfather's craft beer and work hard to get the beer distributed in North America. They were fulfilling an old man's dream, and Penelope didn't want to hurt that dream. "I won't mess up. Promise."

Clara gave her a disbelieving look, and hell, Penelope deserved that look a thousand times over. But then her gaze fell to the bay windows behind the kitchen. "Mason. You need a coat!" She rushed toward the back door, grabbing his winter coat before heading back outside.

"You're my hero," Maisie said with drawl when Clara disappeared out the back door. "Skating on the fountain in high heels. And somehow getting out of a Clara lecture. Amazing."

Penelope ignored Maisie's amusement and whirled around to Amelia. "Seriously, you saw me on YouTube?"

"Oh, yeah, and it was so damn funny," Amelia said, digging her fork into her pie. "We also saw you fawning all over Darryl."

Maisie handed Penelope her phone. The hazy event from the other night appeared on the screen. She wasn't sure what she expected to feel, but she did know one thing. "Hey," Penelope said after a minute. "I *am* pretty damn good in my high heels!"

Amelia laughed and nodded. "I take it things went well with Darryl?"

"Very well," she said. "I think he's actually gotten hotter over the years. How is that even possible?"

Maisie shrugged. "He's probably also happy that a woman from out of town is here. All the well-meaning ladies keep trying to set him up, but it's always with girls totally wrong for him."

"I'm with Maisie on this one," Amelia said. "The poor guy has got two big red Xs against him. Recently divorced. And a cop, meaning he's gotta be the good guy all the time."

"Ha," Penelope said. "I think that good guy thing is all for show. That bad boy could definitely be on the naughty list, especially when you get him naked."

Maisie giggled. "Gross, and yet, I'm happy for you guys. Darryl's sweet, and you deserve some fun over the holidays too." She paused then smiled warmly. "Nothing like rekindling a romance to warm up the winter."

"I wouldn't say we're rekindling anything," Penelope clarified. "It was a moment. We took it." She paused at Amelia giving her a funny look. "What?"

"Oh, nothing," Amelia said slyly, scooping up the pie on her fork. "I'm just wondering if maybe Darryl's the type of guy that could make you stick around and live somewhere longer than a few months."

"No one has that magical power," Penelope said, digging into her pie again. "Especially not a small-town cop who plays by all the rules."

"But didn't you just say he's a bad boy?" Maisie countered.

"Pie," Penelope said, pointing to her plate with her fork. "No more talking, just pie."

Laughter filled the kitchen, and she liked that sound maybe more than she should. Ten years she'd been traveling, road-tripping all over the coast, finding work where her heart told her to stay for a bit. She liked her life. No, she *loved* her adventures. But if she were being honest with herself, this wasn't so bad either. *Home. Family.* And neither was the idea of having more of Darryl.

AN HOUR LATER, Darryl moved toward the desk with the typewriter and grabbed an incident report out of the filing cabinet. Typically, he did these reports the night the incident occurred, but the snowstorm had gotten in his way. Not that he minded. Christ, his muscles were sore, his chest was lighter, and his blood felt like it was pumping through his veins easier. Christmas came early this year, and dammit, history was repeating itself again. Five days he had with Penelope ten years ago. Five days he'd get again. At least this time when she left, he'd get to say goodbye. Though, admittedly, he was still grappling with the real reason *why* she left, and that it wasn't because he'd screwed it up by blurting exactly what he'd been feeling at the time.

A good twenty years before Darryl had become a cop, the River Rock police station had taken ownership of the old courthouse on Main Street with its big white columns outside. Inside the station, the space was modernized with the reception desk at the front near the waiting room. A thin hallway down the left side led to a larger room with beehive desks, some with computers on top, others with typewriters.

When he took a seat at the desk, his captain said from somewhere behind Darryl, "Update on Penelope Carter."

The captain sidled up next to the desk. He was a broody guy, big in the shoulders, and in the center, and his dark eyes matched his typically hard expression.

"Community service during the holiday events," Darryl responded.

"That'll do." The captain went to turn away when he suddenly froze. "Wilson," he said, glancing over his shoulder. "Let's not make it a habit of drooling over the women we take into custody. Remember everyone is looking at you for your promotion."

Darryl sat back in his seat and arched an eyebrow.

"Ms. Carter wasn't the only one seen on that video," the captain pointed out.

It was a rare thing to see amusement in the captain's eyes. Even rarer to see his shoulder's shaking with his laughter as he strode away. Great. The shock at seeing Penelope again, the heat he'd felt for her all those years ago that had taken his damn breath away, returned with a vengeance, and having her close again had brought unexpected intensity.

He didn't need to see the video to know that happened. He'd been there. Experienced it himself.

He put his mind back onto his work and continued typing up the report on Penelope Carter. A 911 call had been made, and Darryl had to write up the report, detailing her community service work, no matter that he didn't want her name anywhere near a police report. And there was no fooling nothing, she remained as much of a problem today as she had the second he saw her. Once, he blew his long-awaited promotion by getting drunk and ending up in a bar fight that placed himself at the center of the town's gossip for weeks. That couldn't happen again. Penelope was the type of girl who skated drunk on fountains. Fun, but not exactly good for his reputation. The higher ups were watching him. He wouldn't regret his night with Penelope. He simply needed it to be only a one-time thing. Soon, she'd leave. Life would go back to normal. He could deal with the loneliness if he had his job. When everything went south with his wife, he always had his work and the respect of the people of the town. He didn't want to sacrifice either.

This year, he'd taken over one of the retiree's positions in the Christmas events to prove he was the right guy for the job. He wanted strictly a day shift to have something that resembled a life, and to get that, he needed the promotion to police sergeant.

When he hit enter to type on the next line, a deep voice said, "Who's the sexy skater?" Jack Fitzpatrick, Natalie's brother and Darryl's long-time buddy, grabbed the chair from the desk next to him and twirled it around, sitting on it backward.

"She's the cousin of the Carter sisters," Darryl replied, using his two index fingers to terribly type out the report.

"Ah, so it *is* Penelope Carter."

Darryl didn't know what Jack meant by that. He didn't care either. What he did care about was the fact that perhaps the whole station had heard about the video. Ignoring the amusement in his friend's light brown eyes, he asked, "How'd you hear about the video?"

"Natalie, actually."

Darryl stopped typing and glanced sideways at his ex-brother-in-law. "She called you?"

"I think you made her day." Jack smiled, thrusting his fingers through his wild brown hair. "Her friend shared the video on Facebook, and she told me that you looked cozy." Jack leaned forward, his eyes all but twinkling. "A little recon later, she discovered the woman was Penelope Carter, the girl you had a crush on during camp one summer."

At that, Darryl froze. "I don't remember ever telling Nat about Penelope."

"In passing, she said." Jack shrugged. "She seemed to know who she was and got all excited. You know how she talks fast and shit."

Darryl shook his head, focusing back on the type-writer, and his job. "She needs to stop worrying about me." He began typing again slowly, ensuring he didn't make any mistakes. "Tell her that I'm fine, and that it's weird for an ex-wife to worry about their ex-husband's love life."

Jack cupped Darryl's shoulder. "Don't think she'll stop that until you marry again."

Most times, ex-spouses had a level of resentment, but that didn't exist between him and Natalie. He loved her in the most platonic way. They stopped having sex way before they broke up, and because of that, a friendship had been borne that made Darryl want her to be happy. Truly happy. Not just half-assing it through life. He'd seen his mother go through hell, never demanding her own happiness. He wouldn't do that to any woman. Especially not a woman that cared about him. "Tell Nat that I'm not with Penelope. She's leaving after Christmas."

"But you're sleeping with her."

Darryl glanced sideways and arched an eyebrow. "Why again is this any of your business?"

Jack paused as a couple of cops strode by and then he grinned. "Because I'm part of the gossip train now and need the goods or my sister will slaughter me."

"Pussy." Darryl laughed, shaking his head and starting to type again. "Are you heading out to Wisconsin tonight for the holidays?"

"Yeah, Heather's packing up the kids now, and we leave in a few hours." Jack and Heather had two cute little ones, a girl and a boy, twenty-one months apart.

"Nice. Say hello to everyone for me." Darryl read what he'd already typed: *PENELOPE CARTER has agreed to ten hours of community service for the inconvenience of the public intoxication.*

"So, give me something." Jack slapped a hand down on the desk. "Nat's going to ask all about this reunion with Penelope."

Even to Darryl, the situation with Natalie could, at times, seem strange. But the truth was, Darryl knew Natalie felt guilty that she had moved on. She was two months pregnant with her new boyfriend's baby, and Darryl was alone.

He was good with alone.

Well, maybe he had been good with the alone before last night. The type of alone that didn't include the greatest sex of his life. The thought of going back to life that didn't include sex wasn't particularly appealing.

He knew Jack wouldn't quit unless he gave him something, so he turned to his best childhood friend. "Unless you want to tell Nat that last night and this morning, I had more sex than we had in the last four years of our marriage, and that the sex was hot as shit, you should tell her there's nothing going on with me and Penelope."

Jack barked a laugh. "Poor Penelope. Surprised she didn't get sick of you after the first time." He paused, the amusement fading. "There's really nothing there anymore?"

Jack had been the only one Darryl had told Penelope. After Nat had left and it became clear that his ex-brother-in-law wasn't going to leave him alone about finding a better match, he'd told Jack about 'the one that got away'. He knew that Darryl risked kissing Penelope, and maybe losing his job, all because he couldn't help himself. He knew that when Penelope left, Darryl blamed himself, thinking he scared her away. And Jack had been the guy that Darryl had talked to when he wondered what she was doing in her life. "All that is happening is all that can. She leaves the day after Christmas."

"You can't convince her to stay?"

"Doubt it would be a good idea." Darryl pulled the report out of the typewriter, giving it a look over, then added, "She's a handful."

"And that's a bad thing?" Jack laughed.

"When you're up for a promotion and everyone is looking at you, yeah, that's a bad thing." Darryl spun his chair to face Jack fully. "It is what it is, then it will end. If you gotta tell Nat anything, tell her *I am fine*." He wasn't sure how many more times he had to say that for everyone to start believing him. Maybe it was because he wasn't saying *I am happy*, but he was never a liar.

"It's a pity Penelope's not staying longer," Jack said and then rose, tucking the chair back under the table.

"Probably for the best, though. Don't think she could handle how much you stink in the summer."

Darryl snorted. But getting razzed by Jack meant that Jack was happy for him in his weird way. "Merry Christmas, dipshit."

Jack squeezed his shoulder. "Merry Christmas, Casanova."

CHAPTER FIVE

"OH, HELL NO," Penelope sputtered, glaring down at the spread for the Christmas breakfast at the River Rock's high school gymnasium the next morning. Scrambled eggs that looked over-scrambled were in big slow cookers on the long table. Sausages that may or may not be made of real meat, toast that had burnt spots, and even the hot chocolate packages that Darryl had given her at his place, lay resting for the person who quite possibly hadn't had a real cooked breakfast in years.

"Problem?" Darryl asked.

She peeled her gaze away from the sorry excuse of a community breakfast to Darryl's warm—albeit con-fused—eyes. When he'd picked her up this morning, she discovered that Darryl looked real good in a Santa Claus hat. "Yes, there is a major problem," she said, pointing to the table. "You call *this* a Christmas breakfast?"

He surveyed the food set out, wearing a plaid button-down overtop a gray shirt, a frown pulling on the sides of his mouth. "It's all that we've got in the budget." He lifted his gaze to hers again with an arched brow. "And sadly, I wouldn't say anyone on the force is much of a chef."

Okay, that was a problem. She was a terrible cook too.

She examined the crowd around her entering the gym, taking a spot at the long tables with plastic chairs set up. When Darryl picked her up this morning, he explained that most of the people they'd be feeding today were having hard times, and yet, all she saw was beaming smiles.

Within those smiles, an idea began to form. She'd promised Clara she wouldn't do anything stupid. And yet...*the fountain.* Maybe she could fix her wrongs by doing something right. "Come with me." She took Darryl's hand then grabbed her Santa Claus hat that she'd been originally reluctant to put on and headed for the gymnasium's door.

Darryl matched her speed, keeping hold of her hand. "Plan on telling me where we're going?"

"Nope."

They quickly made it outside, and the brisk wind hit her face, taking her breath away. She released Darryl's hand to wrap her arms around her sweater, regretting she hadn't grabbed her jacket on the way out the door. She hurried across the street, passing beneath the big snowflake lights hung up on the lamppost. River Rock did one thing well. They knew how to Christmas. The storefronts had a competition every year to win the esteemed *Downtown Christmas River Rock* award, or so Maisie had told Penelope when she noticed the decorated town on her first day there. The effort River Rock's store owners made for a gorgeous Christmas village with garland and lights added so much cheer to the town that the Grinch would've smiled.

One block down, Penelope entered Snowy Mountain Bakery and was hit with the overwhelming aroma of sugar and warmed bread. She rubbed her arms, trying to warm up, moving toward the all-glass counter with the treats inside.

Darryl shut the door behind him, sending the chime above the door to ring, looking like he wasn't cold at all. Of course, he had enough muscles to keep him going all winter long. When he stopped in next to her, he frowned. "We don't have the money for this."

"Maybe the police department doesn't, but I do." Or her father did. He deposited money into her account he set up for her every Christmas, but she never spent the money. It always felt like a terrible apology she never wanted. But if she could help people while also making her cousins look good, that was a total win-win in her books. She hurried to the counter, where a cute-as-a-button elderly lady was working behind the counter with a Christmas apron on and *Susan* written in calligraphy on the front. "Mornin'," Penelope said, without missing a beat. "I'll take it all."

The women blinked. "Pardon me, dear?"

"All this yumminess." Penelope waved out at the glass displays. "I'll take it all." She reached into her back pocket and grabbed the bank card from her wallet. "Oh, and everything in the back if you've got more."

"Um…" The lady blinked rapidly, her purplish curls bouncing atop her head while she twisted and turned. "My dear, I'm not even sure what this would all cost. Annie?" she called toward the back room.

Annie, appearing to be in her early forties, with the same soft brown eyes as Susan, came out of the backroom with a bright smile and a matching Christmas apron. "Good morning."

"Hi." Penelope smiled.

"This kind lady—" The woman looked back at Penelope. "Sorry, dear, what was your name?"

"Penelope Carter."

Susan smiled then said to Annie, "Penelope would like to buy everything we've got. Can you work that out?"

"Really?" Annie asked with wide eyes.

"Really." Penelope nodded, feeling good about being good, which was a rarity.

"Christmas surprises are all around, then." Annie laughed, grabbing a notepad and a pen and following Susan to the far side of the glass display where the most delicious muffins waited.

"This isn't going to be cheap," Darryl said.

"I know." Penelope turned around, finding Darryl watching her with a perplexed expression and his hands shoved in the pockets of his Levi's. "But it's money that I never touch, so it doesn't matter."

One brow winged up. "Let me understand this: You've got money sitting around and you choose to spend that money on baked goods?"

Most times she questioned her own sanity. "It's money that my dad puts into a bank account he created for me," she explained, fully aware of the tightness filling her throat at that admission. "I like to call it his 'guilt money'."

Darryl's head cocked, emotion filling his gaze.

She looked away, trying not to get too lost in the warmth in their depths. "To be perfectly honest, I don't even know how much is in there." *To tell the truth, or not tell the truth?* The old version of herself would've lied through her teeth, not wanting anyone to see the *real* her. She liked the way Darryl spoke openly about his life. He hid nothing. That had to feel good. Back in control of her emotions, she faced him. "I promised Clara that I wouldn't do anything stupid while I was here. You know, with them trying to make the brewery a success, and well…"

"The fountain," he offered with a grin.

"The fountain." She smiled. "So, this is a good thing, right? Better food for the people of River Rock. I'm a Carter so that will look good on the family." She paused as Annie finished emptying the first glass cabinet and had moved onto the next, before addressing Darryl again. "I figure the more good I do before Clara finds out I'm on YouTube—because she's legit going to murder me—the better."

Darryl cocked his head, studying her intently like she was a curious puzzle.

"What?"

He started at her intently. "I don't think you realize what this gesture will do."

Doing good things meant happy people, didn't it? "What do you mean?"

He wrapped an arm around her waist and pulled up against his warmth. He dropped his chin and his mouth came close to hers, his minty breath brushing across her lips. "The people of River Rock are going to fall madly and hopelessly in love with you."

"Is that a bad thing?" she asked, pressing her arms against his strong chest, lost in those warm eyes.

His mouth twitched. "Depends on how much you like to be loved."

She pondered. Then the truth fell from her mouth. "You know what, being loved too much has got to be a whole lot better than disappointing people all the time."

"You're right, it does." He lifted his hand to her face, then, his fingers gently sliding across her cheek. "You're a good woman, Penelope. Don't let anyone make you believe otherwise."

Her heart squeezed, threatening to turn into mush. Okay, sure, she hadn't been doing all this for someone to tell her that she didn't suck. But she liked hearing his praise. "Now, don't you go make me cry, Darryl Wilson. That's not very Christmas-y at all."

He slowly shook his head. "Wouldn't dare think of it."

"Besides, I'm doing this to right an already made wrong," she pointed out. "Not the noblest of causes."

He hesitated then nodded, like he couldn't be swayed to believe otherwise. "A good cause, nonetheless."

"Says the cop who dragged my drunk ass off a fountain," she said, snort laughing.

His heated gaze scanned her lips before returning to her eyes again. That intense regard was something she remembered over the years. When Darryl looked at anything, he *really* looked, especially when that thing was a person. She'd never met anyone after him that seemed to give her so much attention. Maybe that's what made Darryl a good cop. He cared deeply. He paid attention. He saw the little things others missed.

Whatever it was, she liked that about him. In a sea of feeling like no one understood her, and even sometimes her not understanding herself, there was Darryl. A very good man who thought she was *good* too, no matter what she'd done.

"You know," he said, eventually breaking the silence. "I have seen people at their worst. I've seen people do unthinkable things. You might be trouble—that goes without saying—but you don't have a bad bone in you." His strength, his heat, it all engulfed her when he wrapped his arms around her tight. "Regardless that you're doing this for a reason, *you* thought of it. Give yourself some credit, Penelope."

Maybe she was being too hard on herself...*maybe*... "Okay, then maybe I will." She smiled at him then set her gaze on the two women filling the boxes of cinnamon buns, cakes, pastries, and so much more.

People loved Christmas. The warmth of it. The magic. Penelope didn't know why exactly, but she had a feeling this was one step closer to finding out.

MOST PEOPLE DIDN'T surprise Darryl. He had a knack for reading people, most times seeing right through them. Penelope surprised the hell out of him. Sure, over the years, he had wondered about the girl that captivated him intently during those five days at camp. She'd been so full of life, then. Unlike any girl he'd met before. And when he kissed her, he hadn't regretted it. The kiss had felt *right*. But today, he saw a different side of Penelope, a softer side, a sweeter side. He liked that side, as much as he liked how she didn't seem to take life too seriously.

Damn. He could use a little of that in his very routine world.

The Christmas breakfast had gone off without a hitch, and the two hours after they had returned from the bakery, he knew that not only was his first Christmas event a huge success, but Penelope had made it so. Behind the large table, he had finished cleaning out the crockpots after packaging up boxes of food for anyone that wanted to take it with them, since most people there filled up on the treats from the bakery. He finished packing up one slow cooker in a box, settling it next to the others, and then found Penelope hugging Al, a war veteran who had many rough times in his life. An odd warmth carried through Darryl watching the exchange. She'd grown into a fine woman. A good woman. Kind in ways that he began believing not many knew about her.

When Penelope waved a final goodbye to Al, she caught Darryl looking at her, and gave him that bright smile. She wore jeans and flat shoes and a bright red sweater that happened to hug her body in ways he couldn't ignore. Matched with that Santa hat atop her head, Darryl couldn't help but wonder what she'd look like naked wearing only that hat.

She finally reached him, and asked, "Do I pass at my first community service event, Officer Wilson?"

"With flying colors, Ms. Carter," he said with a smile.

Her lips parted but then a soft voice interjected, "Oh, my dear, you are just the sweetest thing River Rock has ever seen." Mrs. Evans, a retired kindergarten teacher, smiled at Penelope, sidling up to her. "Keep this to stay warm." She wrapped a knitted scarf around Penelope's neck, whose eyes suddenly widened. "And for that beautiful heart of yours."

Penelope blinked rapidly, glancing from Darryl to Mrs. Evans. "Thank you, but honestly, this was nothing."

"To you, maybe not, dear, but look at those smiles." Mrs. Evan gestured at the crowd sitting at the tables, laughing and enjoying the baked goods. "The joy you brought them today is a very real and big thing."

Penelope's mouth opened then shut.

Darryl smiled, leaning against the table behind him and folding his arms. Being surprised looked good on her.

"Mrs. Evans hit the nail on the head with that statement," Jason, the man who ran the homeless shelter across town, said. He offered his hand to Penelope. "What you did today, Penelope, was kind and generous, and I'm not sure I could say enough thank-yous to repay this."

"No repayment needed," she said, wringing her fingers together, obviously uncomfortable with the compliments.

Sad. Penelope was this bright light, exuding life, and he wondered how a woman like this wasn't told everyday how incredible she was? Which, in turn, made him feel like the world's biggest asshole. He'd done what maybe everyone in her life had done: expected that she would screw up in some epic way, and somehow her fuckup would make him look bad.

His gut told him that Penelope was greatly misunderstood. He'd been wrong to judge her. He intended to fix that too.

Darryl said his goodbyes to Mrs. Evans and Jason after Penelope did.

When they were alone again, Penelope turned to him. "Okay, so you weren't kidding about how the townsfolk would be." She gave an easy laugh, stuffing her hands into her pockets. "Good grief, it's like I saved the town from aliens or something."

"They're just a kind bunch," Darryl explained. "They like to acknowledge good people." Though she had no idea what she started. "But trust me, you haven't seen anything. Word hasn't even hit the street yet."

The color drained from her face. She sputtered something incoherent then said clearly, "Okay, remember when I said I'm not really big into the whole Christmas cheer thing?"

"Yeah."

"I meant that."

He laughed. Damn, she was cute. "I'm sure you did, but around here, Christmas is everything. They'll treat you like you're this year's Christmas angel."

She cringed. "It was *baked goods.*"

He leaned in and dropped his gaze to her eye level, inhaling that sweet scent only belonging to her. "I never said they couldn't be a bit much, at times." He chuckled to himself and then moved to the rest of the slow cookers and began packing those up in the boxes to return to his fellow cops who had lent them. Penelope settled in next to him, her arm brushing his. With that simple touch, heat filled his groin. His plan had been to keep things platonic today, ensuring nothing could go wrong with his promotion, but with that heat tempting him, and seeing this new side of her, he asked, "Got any plans tonight?"

She closed the box. "Maisie was talking about watching sappy Christmas movies all night."

"How about I give you a pass on that?" He rose and dropped his gaze to her as she stayed on her knees. Weakness flooded him, followed by hot desire to see her right there when they were both naked.

"What kind of pass?" she breathed, obviously reacting to the heat tormenting him.

"Come away with me somewhere for the night."

"Hmmm." She slowly rose until her soft curves were pressed against his hard planes. "And pass up Christmas movies…I don't know, that's a real tough one."

He grinned, tucking her hair behind her ear. "What if I promise you that tonight will be more romantic than those sappy Christmas movies?"

She slid her hands up his biceps. "That's a hefty promise." Need coursed through him, and he brought his mouth close to hers.

Right as his lips brushed across hers, a surprised voice said, "I don't believe it."

He glanced sideways finding Clara. For a moment, he thought Clara was surprised about Darryl nearly kissing Penelope. He quickly realized that he had it all wrong when Clara added, "You did all this, Penelope?"

"God, no," Penelope gasped, taking a step back, her cheeks notably flushed. "Darryl put this event on. I just helped by getting some treats at the bakery."

Clara watched her cousin for a long moment then placed her hands onto her hips. "That's it. Fess up, what in the hell is going on here? Why are you helping with this? I thought you hated Christmas."

Darryl quickly turned away and went for the next slow cooker to stay the hell out of this conversation. The last thing he wanted to do was put Penelope in the hot seat with her cousin, considering she'd done so great today. But he also knew Clara from high school. She was one tough cookie. Clara had dated his best friend in high school, Sullivan Kenne. He'd moved away when the National Baseball League signed him, but Darryl had seen Clara back then—she had a huge heart beneath all that toughness. Her annoyance at Penelope was pure worry.

"There's nothing up," Penelope defended. "Can't a person just help out?"

Behind Darryl's back, Amelia's voice joined in. "I think it's so great, Penelope. Seriously, way to go. You're the talk of the town."

Clara's voice softened, just enough to warm. "And it's really true? You bought out the bakery?"

"Yeah, I bought some baked goods," Penelope said quickly. "No biggie. People are making way too much out of this. God, it's not like I saved a baby from a burning building or something."

"It's a very kind thing to do," Clara said, obvious pride in her voice. "So, hurry up and get over here and hug me." There was some shuffling around, and then Clara added, "You made us all super proud today."

"Well, ah, I'm glad," Penelope said tightly.

Darryl smiled to himself and shut the box, suddenly aware of the heavy silence at his back. Feeling all the laser-focused feminine eyes watching him, he drew in a deep breath then turned to them and smiled. "Hi, ladies."

Clara's hard expression slid back into place. "We all set for the barn dance on Christmas Eve?"

He nodded. "We are." Three Chicks Brewery was donating beer to the barn dance to raise money for the literacy program at the school. Darryl suspected for Amelia and Maisie, the move was about donating to their town, but for Clara, he didn't doubt in the least she thought of the donation as smart business. Which it was. "I'll send some of the guys over to help load up the kegs, if that works."

She nodded, warmth filling her gaze. "We'd appreciate the help." She turned to Penelope. "We'll see you at home later?"

"You will." She smiled.

"Mommy, donuts."

Clara spun around. "No, those are for—"

Darryl smiled, watching her hightail it after Mason who was beelining toward the pastry table.

Amelia rolled her eyes. "He takes after his aunts. He loves sugar. I don't know why she denies him such deliciousness."

Penelope laughed and waved at Amelia before she walked away.

"He's a handful," Penelope said, turning back to Darryl. "But damn is he a cute handful."

"Like someone else I know too." He winked.

Penelope gave a sweet smile before turning back to Clara, who snatched her son up the moment he shoved a donut into his mouth. "A fast handful too," he said with a dry laugh.

"She's a good mom, though," Penelope said. "I don't know how she does it all on her own."

"Single moms are the strongest women I know." His mother included.

Penelope nodded then packed up another Crock-Pot.

"No kid or mother deserves a deadbeat father," Darryl added, staring at Mason, whose cheeks looked like a hamster's full of food. Every time Darryl looked at the kid, he felt like he was looking at his best childhood friend. "I once thought my buddy Sully was Mason's father."

Penelope turned to him with wide eyes. "Clara's ex?"

Darryl nodded. "Mason looks like him." Had from day one, and that still hadn't changed. "I confronted Clara once to see if Sullivan wasn't doing the right thing by her. I was ready to go to Boston and knock some damn sense into him, if that was the case."

"What did Clara say?" Penelope asked.

Darryl recalled that tense conversation. "Clara told me that Mason wasn't Sullivan's. That she'd been with someone she had met right after they broke up, and he didn't want a child."

"What a bastard," Penelope clipped.

Darryl watched Clara go down to one knee and talk sternly to the boy. He still wasn't convinced the child wasn't Sullivan's. Mason had his friend's eyes.

"You don't believe her, do you?"

Darryl jerked his gaze to Penelope, finding her watching him closely. "It's not my place to believe or not believe her." He'd told Sullivan about Mason, not once, but twice, and Sullivan had called Clara. Darryl didn't know the outcome of that call. It wasn't his business to ask. "She's a great mom," Darryl added. "He's a lucky kid. That's all that matters."

"Yeah, I guess you're right." Penelope gave him a sweet smile. After a long look, she finally exhaled deeply. "Yes."

He frowned, trying to catch up. "Yes?"

"Yes, I'll go with you tonight."

"Ah." He took her hand and tugged her close. "I won over the Christmas movies, then?"

That addictive heat returned to her eyes in a flash, and she pressed her warmth against him, all soft and perfect. "Definitely."

BY THE TIME evening rolled around, Penelope had finished her laundry, had dinner with her cousins, and packed an overnight bag. She got momentarily distracted by a text from her mother.

Your gifts to the kids haven't arrived yet. Did you get them to the post office on time?

Penelope found the tracking number and confirmed the order before texting back. Delivery says it'll arrive by tomorrow morning.

Her mother's response was immediate. You really shouldn't leave these things until the last minute, Penelope.

Penelope didn't respond after that. What would she say? First, they were her half-siblings that she barely even knew. They probably wouldn't even recognize her face out of a picture or know her name. She was like that aunt that only visited every handful of years. And second, the only one who gave her anything for Christmas was her father, and that was money she never wanted. She still had yet to figure out why she needed to participate in Christmas when they made sure not to involve her. Mom obviously wanted to look like she had a perfect happy family to her friends, no doubt.

Her heart clenched tight, not allowing her mother's coldness to affect her. Most times, Penelope could shut out that pain. She'd learned to turn off her emotions and carry on with life. When her internal protective wall fell, she ended up skating drunk on fountains. Not wanting to let her good mood become spoiled, Penelope turned off her phone and ignored the world. Most of all, her family.

It wasn't long after that Darryl had gathered her for their night away, and when she slid onto the passenger seat of his truck, she was sick of the word *thank you*. Sure, her heart warmed knowing she had brought the people of River Rock so much joy, but she wasn't expecting to be highlighted on River Rock's Twitter page. And when she'd folded laundry that afternoon, hiding from the world to catch her breath, the townsfolk stopped in to say thanks. Apparently, River Rock was the town of *nice* people. Which she guessed shouldn't be a surprise. The town was small and quaint, and everyone seemed to know each other, but that was just the opposite of what she knew. Most of the people she knew were transient workers or tourists who never stayed for more than a few days. And she knew why she was drawn to those types of people—having no one in her life permanently was way less scary than letting people in.

The country music played through the speakers as Darryl's truck lights showed off the glistening snowy night. Up ahead, a plow threw dirt onto the snow banks ahead of them, the yellow light on top of the truck nearly blinding.

"You're not afraid of snowmobiles, are you?" Darryl asked, breaking the silence.

She glanced sideways, watching the relaxed way he

drove on their three-hour drive into the wilderness. Yeah, he kinda proved already he could handle just about anything he faced. "Are you kidding me?" She guffawed. "I'm not scared of anything." Okay, maybe letting herself be vulnerable, but he didn't need to know that. "Where are we going, anyway?"

"Now *that's* a surprise." His mouth twitched.

A surprise, huh? She couldn't remember the last time anyone surprised her—if ever. She crossed her legs, staring out at the mesmerizing snow in the truck's headlights as they climbed the summit.

When they finally reached the top, Darryl turned into a driveway that led to a cabin in what defined a postcard-perfect winter getaway. The log cabin was hugged by a mature forest of evergreen trees. With all the lights in the cabin turned on, the floor-to-ceiling triangular windows all but glowed, welcoming anyone into its warmth. "Geez, this place is gorgeous." When he stopped the truck, she hurried out into the brisk cold night, lifting her scarf that she'd received today a little higher onto her neck.

"It's been in my family for generations," he explained. "Passed down, and now belongs to me and Ashley."

Penelope took in the lights again, a sudden realization hitting her. "I thought you said your sister is in England."

"She is." Darryl pressed a strong hand against her back, leading her up to the front door, with their two bags in one hand. "I automated the cabin a couple years ago to switch the lights on and turn up the heat remotely so we're good to go when we come."

"Convenient," she said, kinda impressed by that. She could barely get her life together. Darryl seemed to be so far ahead of the game.

Once she followed him in, she found a quaint cabin, with a cute and cozy living room with a big white faux fur rug in front of the stone fireplace and a brown leather couch. At the far back was a small galley kitchen and an island with tall chairs. The bathroom was set next to the staircase that had a loft-style bedroom.

Darryl dropped their bags near the couch. "You can marvel over the cabin later. I've got a surprise waiting for you." He moved to the coat tree near the front door. "This is all Ashley's stuff." He handed her an armful of snow gear, including snow pants and big winter boots. "You're about the same size."

Well, no, Ashely was a size smaller, but Penelope squeezed into the gear as Darryl easily got into his.

"Ready?" he asked once he finished.

She nodded, wrapping her scarf around her face up to her nose. "Ready."

He led her outside to the small shed off to the right side of the house. After he vanished inside, an engine roared to life, followed by him exiting and pushing a snowmobile. He offered her a helmet before he fastened his own.

"Good to go?" he asked.

She gave a big thumbs-up with her enormous mittens.

He adjusted her scarf until all that showed was her eyes. "It's a cold one." He grabbed his face scarf, placing it over his nose, then he got on the snowmobile and she settled in behind him.

She wrapped her arms around him tight, and then they were off. Apart from feeling like a giant pillow in her snow gear, the ride was incredible. The moon was bright along the journey, guiding their way, as did the light on the snowmobile. Darryl obviously knew the area well as he went a decent speed through the forest on a snow-covered trail until the snowmobile slowed.

When he stopped and cut the ignition, she got off and glanced out at the frozen pond, unable to believe her eyes. She moved closer, squinting at the lights she could see on the other side. The rows of cabins, with lights on inside.

"Is this…?" She could barely get the words out.

Darryl stepped closer. "Our spot."

She pulled her scarf aside then glanced into the warmth of his eyes. His face mask was down, and she could see his breath was quick, like her own. Unable to find words to explain the emotion squeezing at her heart, she glanced around and spotted the big large boulder. Not much had changed in the area in the ten years she'd been there except the snow that covered the ground. "You kissed me right here." She turned around and sat on the rock, exactly like she had that one warm night.

Darryl smiled, identical to that night she had never been able to forget. As he strode toward her, reality flickered, the past returning like no time had passed by at all.

God, Darryl was hot. Lean, and his hair was so messy and wild, with eyes that melted her bones. While she loved her summers in River Rock with her cousins, it providing a nice break from all the yelling and fighting at home between her parents, she never expected to find Darryl. He'd been the best surprise of getting the job as a camp counselor she never wanted but her aunt forced her to get.

Darryl brought heat and intensity with him as he approached her with purposeful steps, and that curve of his mouth told her he was coming in for a kiss. She wanted his kiss.

"You're going to get me fired," he said. "We both could get fired for this."

"It's fun to live on the wild side." She smiled, all for show. Holy shit, holy shit, holy shit. This was so happening. She slowly pressed herself against the boulder behind her. "And I know you want me as much as I want you." Five days they'd had together, flirting, laughing, and teasing each

other. The best five days of her life.

He licked his lips, watching her mouth. "You're right. I do want you."

She nibbled her bottom lip then crossed her legs, squeezing her thighs against the building warmth and wetness. "Then what are you waiting for? Kiss me."

Heat flared in his eyes, and she burned all over when he closed the distance and pressed his lips against hers. His mouth was soft and yet held strength too. He wrapped his one arm around her, then his mouth opened ever so slightly until his tongue brushed against hers. He held her tight, showing her the way with his gentle mouth, and she didn't want him to ever stop.

But then he did.

And when he broke away, she felt breathless and light-headed. "Not bad for our first kiss," she joked.

He wasn't smiling. He stared at her with an intensity she'd never known. "Believe me, Penelope, stick with me, and I'll make our first everything incredible." Desire simmered between them before his mouth met hers again. He kissed her harder this time, more demanding. His tongue thrust into her mouth. His fingers tightened around her ponytail, and when he deepened the kiss, a needy sound escaped her mouth that she'd never heard before.

One she wanted to make again. And louder. She wiggled against all his hardness, never wanting him to stop.

But then he did. And when he drew away, his gaze burned hot and possessive. "Damn, girl, you make me want to kiss you every day for the rest of my life."

When Darryl's fingers gripped her chin, she returned to the *now*, and she stared into the eyes of a *man* not a boy. "This is where I kissed you, just like this. Do you remember?"

Something inside of her shifted, a pang in her heart flickered, when he brought his lips close to hers. "I remember everything," she whispered.

Then his lips met hers, and the kiss was different, more emotion packed than when they were younger. She fell into the kiss, feeling like they'd somehow dropped into a time warp. They were the same people, but different. *She* was different, and she wasn't exactly sure how she felt about who she was now, if maybe somehow she'd lost her way these past few years.

Once she believed in love, and she knew that all those years ago when her mom dragged her from camp to announce their divorce, she stopped believing and became a person who ran from anything serious.

But now, in this moment, she felt good about his kiss.

So damn good.

She didn't want him to stop kissing her, but he did. He leaned away and smiled softly. "Just as I remember it."

She mirrored his smile to hide the emotions flaring in her chest.

He let out a long breath, creating a cloud of white between them when he stepped back to settle on the rock next to her, and glanced out to the lake. "It's amazing how much things have changed in the ten years since we were here before."

She brought up one knee, resting her chin on top. "So much has changed, hasn't it?" Maybe that's what bothered her most. She wasn't sure she liked how she'd changed. Really, what had she done in those ten years? *Nothing.* "Any regrets?" she asked.

"No," he answered without hesitation. "Things happened because they needed to." His gaze fell to hers. "And we're back here again, aren't we?"

"We are," she managed through her thick throat.

A long moment passed as she stared out at the cabins that had been the last place she'd ever felt at home until now. Everything had changed after she left camp. She changed. She could barely remember that innocent girl back then who didn't know anything about pain. The one who believed in love.

"How about you?" he asked. "Any regrets?"

She drew in a long deep breath, finding the answer an easy one to give. "I regret that I'm not the same girl that sat on this rock ten years ago."

He went unnaturally still. "What girl is that?"

"The girl that thought love was easy." She hesitated then opened her heart. "The girl that believed a parent could love you above all else. The girl that believed that fate would always lead you to the right place, as long as you were a good person. The girl that believed in the damn fairytale."

She thought Darryl might give her the same answer that everyone did—love *was* easy. Or some other platitude she didn't believe, but he didn't. He said, "Love is fucked up, and can fuck you up, but sometimes it's all about finagling your way through it until you find something that makes you happy…whatever that may be."

When her throat tightened with emotion, she looked away, and he added, "You don't deserve the way your parents hurt you, Penelope."

She forced a smile. "What's the saying? Something can only hurt you if you let it."

"That's a hard lesson when it's coming from your parents." He nudged her shoulder with his. "And I should know since I have a bastard of a father that walked out on us and never came back."

Silence fell between them.

She drew in another long breath, staring out at the cabins. She supposed there was some truth behind what he said. She only got one shot at this crazy thing called life. Maybe it was time to stop running and find that *thing* that made her happy. "Ever wonder what would have happened if I hadn't been ripped away that day?"

she asked him.

He wrapped his arm around her. "I wondered that every day the whole rest of the summer. And then, although I'm ashamed to admit it, sometimes even when I was with Nat."

Somehow, she didn't need to hear more than that. Because life *did* happen. Everything changed that night he kissed her. The life she had was forever different in so many ways. What she believed of love and loyalty was tossed away. And she was left to glue her own self together. But she never forgot the kiss or the guy who wanted to be her first everything.

Darryl.

She dropped her head on his shoulder. "You did it, you know."

"What did I do?"

"You totally *are* better than a Christmas movie."

His laughter echoed across the lake, and she smiled with him, feeling like it was perhaps the most honest smile she'd had in ten years.

CHAPTER SIX

THE RIDE BACK to the cabin had been bitterly cold with the brisk wind hitting Darryl's face. Penelope hung on tight, thankfully blocked by his torso. She'd been quiet for a while at the lake, and he'd wondered what weighed so heavily on her mind. Probably her terrible fucking parents. They didn't deserve her. He barely knew her and still could figure that out. When they finally made it back to the cabin, she'd remained closed off, and even after he built a fire, she sat on the couch, staring at the flames, silently in her own mind.

He couldn't take it anymore. After he got the fire roaring, he turned to her and asked gently, "Why so quiet?"

She drew in a long deep breath before looking away from the fire toward him. Her expression showed very little. "Just thinking."

"About?" he pressed.

"About how different life was when we had those five days together," she eventually said. "We were so young, so free, all of our dreams ahead of us."

"You are still young," he reminded her, "and if I may say, very much free."

Her eyes warmed with her laugh, and she shook her head. "It's different."

"How so?"

"Maybe I'm more jaded now," she offered, obviously not fearful of stating the truth. "Definitely more aware that my life isn't what I thought it'd be."

At that, he cocked his head, very curious over *that* statement. "Your life isn't what you want it to be?"

"No, I mean…" She inhaled sharply then sent her gaze onto the fire, neatly avoiding him. "My life is fine. I love traveling, seeing the world, and all that stuff." The orange hues from the fire cast a soft glow on her face, showing off the gentle lines of her cheekbones. "Tonight, it's just…I don't know…I got little pieces of the girl I was back then. Before that night, I lived in this bubble, you know, where life was perfect and happy, and I thought anything was possible. Sometimes I wish I could go back to that girl."

His heart reached for her. Fuck, did it ever. Because he remembered that girl too. "You're as vivacious as you were back then, still strong and sexy and bold."

She smiled softly. "But…?"

He paused. "Honestly?"

"Why not?"

"There is one subtle difference I see in you," he said

softly, unsure if speaking the truth would bite him in the ass later. "The girl I met at camp wouldn't have run. Not from anything." She quickly glanced away, and he knew he'd hit a nerve, but he also knew it was probably true. "Your strength back then had been mind-boggling to me. I remember thinking that you weren't a leader. You also weren't a follower. You were just…Penelope, this force to be reckoned with that had me kissing her when I could lose my job. And I *never* broke the rules, that's not who I was back then, nor who I am now." He spotted her rapid blinking and welling eyes, and added, "And I liked that Penelope. A lot."

"You were twenty-years-old. We only spent five days together," she said with a roll of her eyes to obviously hide her tears.

He moved to her and knelt in front of the couch. She held his gaze when he cupped her chin. "I *still* like that Penelope. As much as I like this one."

"You don't even know me anymore," she whispered.

With that line, he suddenly realized that he understood her completely. She wasn't running from shit—she simply couldn't believe in the things she had before. Life had done its damage, like it had on so many people, but on her, that damage seemed…*wrong*. "I know what you show me, and that's certainly enough for me to like what I see."

She smiled softly then, but the warmth never reached

her eyes. "If only everyone saw what you see."

He didn't have words for her, no matter how bad he wanted them. Some people were assholes. Her parents fell into that category, so did his father, a man he hadn't seen since he'd walked out on them. If Darryl knew anything, he knew he hated that selfish pricks made *this* woman feel anything but loved. Desperately wanting to fill that void, he leaned in and waited for her lips to part in invitation before he sealed his mouth against hers. She moaned, moving closer, her arms wrapping around his neck. He gathered her then and laid her out on the rug in front of the crackling fire. "Do you know what I do know about you?"

"What's that?" she asked, her soft eyes on his. Eyes that if he looked deep enough had changed from the time he'd known her as a teenager. But eyes that still spoke to him like they had all those years ago. He liked the soul in them. Christ, that soul was so damn bright, she shined. He sealed his mouth across hers to prove a point, kissing her, hard and demanding, unable to stop the way his body yearned to be near hers. When he leaned away, he stated, "I know how when I kiss you like this, your cheeks get pink and your eyes appear to turn darker." He dropped his mouth to her neck and slid his tongue up its length, and she wiggled under him causing him to smile. "And I know how much you like that spot right there."

"Darryl." She gasped, reaching for his shirt. He helped her remove it over his head, then he kissed her neck again, inhaling the sugary aroma that drove him to near madness. Overwhelmed by the need to make her *feel* something good, he pushed up her shirt, placing butterfly kisses along her sides and her stomach until he pulled her shirt off then quickly unhooked her bra, freeing her completely. He paid attention to her cues, loving how she arched her back every time he sucked on a nipple, urged on by the soft moans she gave. He continued to kiss his way down her body until he flicked open her jeans. She lifted her hips as he pulled them and her panties down over her legs until he had her bared, completely for *him*. He slid his hand up her thigh as he opened the button of his jeans, then he paused only momentarily while he shed the rest of his clothing, exposing his hard cock.

He stroked himself, feeling the urgency running through him. "And I know what you want most of all right now, don't I?"

"You," she rasped, her hair a beautiful blanket beneath her head.

The flames flickered golden light across her taut nipples and round breasts. He stroked his hand across her nipple then squeezed her breast before running his hand down the center of her chest.

"Yeah, and goddamn it, Penelope, do I want you

too." He kissed her, hard, demanding, asking for so much because he knew she'd give it to him. His fingers glided across the warmth of her thigh to her buttock where he squeezed her cheek, grinding his hard length against her sex.

But tonight, he wanted all of her. For himself. To feel her. To taste her. He wanted to memorize every inch of her, so he didn't forget her when she was gone. He wanted to give her something that apparently no one had given her in the last ten years. Attention. He wanted to make her the center of his world.

Overwhelmed by her, he began kissing her neck, loving how she squirmed with every touch. He kissed down her stomach, slowly looking up at her, finding her chest rising and falling with her quick breaths, her chin pointed up to the ceiling. When he settled between her thighs, he lifted her legs onto his shoulders. He drew in her musky scent before he slid the flat of his tongue across the smooth wet flesh. "I won't forget the way you taste," he told her, watching her as she arched her back.

He played right there, with gentle strokes, and sometimes firmer touches, learning her likes and dislikes. Until he had every part of her read, then he sucked on her clit and she lifted her hips in invitation. He slid a finger inside her and then another, and then in rhythm with his tongue, he worked her pleasure, reading every move, following the flow of her body, until she showed him how to get her there.

And damn did he get her there.

She came against his mouth with a beautiful shudder and a perfect moan.

While she lay there, a boneless, sexy woman, he sheathed himself with a condom from his wallet. As she began to open her eyes, he moved his body atop hers, poised at her entrance. He kissed her, bringing heat back into her lithe body. The addictive heat he'd discovered between them, a heat he'd unknowingly been chasing since the night his lips met hers. She wiggled, bringing him deeper inside her, and his mouth froze on hers. He lifted himself up on his forearms, staring into the depths of her eyes.

That's where he wanted to look. Right there. In the eyes of the woman, who as a girl made herself unforgettable. And made him act different than he'd acted before. The woman who had him thinking about her for years after she'd left.

He thrust hard to claim her. Her hands came to his flexed biceps. Her moans drifting around him, her pretty face, her mouth forming a perfect O, her widening eyes, it all brought him more pleasure than he thought he could endure.

Every minute seemed hotter. Every thrust harder. Faster.

Soon the intensity became too much. He strained to

hold onto his control with each hard, fast thrust, getting them both there, but when her climax hit, her inner walls strangling his shaft, her loud screams filling his ears, his pleasure hit with no warning. He thrust again, emptying himself with a low groan that left him dropping his weight onto her.

When he finally had the strength to move off her, he withdrew his softening cock, rolling onto his back, and tucked her against his chest. The crackling fire and his own racing heart were all he heard when she finally wiggled against him, getting closer and more comfortable.

His mind slowly cleared, and with it came a thought he hadn't really remembered until right now. "I wished for you to come back, you know."

She lifted her head, her hair unruly, her lips puffy. "You did?"

He nodded, fixing her hair with a soft laugh. "After you left, we went to this wishing well with the camp. I tossed a penny in, and *you* were what I wished for." He paused, knowing he was throwing a lot out there with this statement. "And you came back."

"Ten years later," she said, placing her head back onto his shoulder.

He slid his hand down her side, resting his touch on the warmth of her hip. "Ten years later is better than never."

A long pause followed, a heavy kind of silence between them. Until Penelope broke it. "If we're admitting truths here, after my parents told me they were getting divorced, when things were bad, like, really, really bad, I wrote a letter to you."

He tucked a finger under her chin, lifting her gaze to his, needing to see her eyes. "You did?"

"I know, totally lame," she said with a laugh. "But I was still seventeen years old, and we did stuff like that."

Now *this* interested him. "What did the letter say?"

"Just that I wanted you to come and get me and bring me back to River Rock." She gave him a cute smile. "Silly, right?"

He released her to tip his head back a moment, the warmth of her naked flesh against his. So many what-ifs, what-could-have-beens. "You should have sent it." He glanced at her again, finding her eyes right on him. "I would have come for you."

She snorted a laugh. "You would've probably thought I was stalking you."

He didn't laugh, unsure why sudden tension filled him. Though as she snuggled her warmth against him, he got his answer. He dropped his lips to the top of her head, inhaling her sweet sugary scent, knowing full well, he wouldn't have thought that. He would have gone after her.

CHAPTER SEVEN

"I'M NOT SURE I can do this."

Darryl glanced down next to him at Penelope, finding her digging her heels in a little. Yeah, he got that. Coming to the pediatric wing of the hospital had been hard for him the first time too, and he had come out of choice. This was the second day of her community service, and he was desperately trying not to think about the fact that tomorrow was Christmas Eve, and soon she'd been gone again. But he wasn't at the hospital to think about himself, or his problems that seemed minuscule in comparison to what the children faced there. "You can do this," he told her gently, reaching for her hand. Her fingers tightened around his. He tried not to think about how good that felt. "Trust me, they are about a thousand times stronger than you or me." He flicked his chin toward Tyson. "And he'll totally make their day."

Penelope drew in a long, deep breath, glanced at the little girl in the hospital room, then gave a firm nod.

He exhaled a little himself to gather the nervousness

that always filled him at the hospital. It wasn't the antiseptic scent stifling the air or the beeping machines; what tightened his gut was always hoping he didn't do something to make a tough situation worse. They passed an empty bed in the hallway then entered the next door on the left. Tyson charged in, reindeer antlers attached to his head, and the little bells rang with every thunderous step forward.

"A puppy," the little girl with the blue beanie cap exclaimed.

Tyson jumped on her bed, somehow always knowing to stay at the end, clear of any tubes.

"Hi, Emily, I'm Darryl," he said, letting go of Tyson's leash so he could inch his way forward to the girl's open arms. "This is Penelope." Warmth filled his chest, erasing the earlier tightness. "And the guy kissing your nose is Tyson."

"He's so cute," the little girl said as Tyson licked her face, sending her giggling.

"Thank you so much for bringing Tyson by," the girl's mother said from her seat next to the bed.

Darryl noticed how little she looked in the bed, and how tired the mother appeared, but he refused to allow the sadness to fill his mind. That was a place he couldn't go to anymore, not if he wanted to stay in his job. He could bring light to their day—and sometimes, that meant that day was a good day. "Tyson wouldn't take no for answer. He's here to pick up Emily's letter for Santa."

The girl's mother reached over on the table. "We've got that right here, all ready to go."

Emily petted Tyson's head, and he dropped his chin down onto her legs, laying like a blanket over her. "Can we take a picture of him?" Emily asked with big bright blue eyes.

Darryl smiled. "Tyson is yours for the next half hour. Take as many as you like."

"Really?" Emily beamed.

Darryl nodded. "Santa's treat to you for being such a good and brave girl this year."

Emily smiled then hugged Tyson around his neck.

Out of the corner of his eye, Darryl noticed Penelope sidle up to him. "Actually," she said, drawing everyone's attention, "I think we can do one better. Can I borrow that paper there and pencil crayons?"

"Oh, sure, of course," Emily's mother said, gathering the items and handing them to Penelope.

Penelope scooted around to the other side of the bed, and sat on the very end, cross-legged, like she belonged there. And for whatever reason, that caused Emily to smile, making Darryl wonder if people were too careful around her. Penelope was anything but careful, probably exactly the type of person Emily would love to be around now.

It suddenly occurred to him that because Penelope

lived in the moment, maybe she understood Emily in ways Darryl simply couldn't.

"Tell me all about your favorite things," Penelope said with a smile, the sketchbook up, hidden from Emily.

Emily played with Tyson's big floppy ears. "I love tacos and sunshine…oh, and the beach…how it's squishy in your toes…"

Darryl tried to keep listening to every word Emily said, but he became lost in how Penelope talked to the little girl. Yeah, Darryl was good with playing with kids. He'd always liked them, hoping to have a few ankle biters of his own one day. But *talking* and *listening*…that was something else entirely.

And Penelope excelled in this area. She paid attention to the girl. Asking all the right questions. Garnering a bright sparkle in Emily's eyes from the conversation.

Ten minutes later, Penelope placed the pencil down next to her. "Okay, I think I'm done." She spun the sketchbook around.

Emily's mom gasped, eyes filling up. "Oh, wow, Emmy, look how beautiful that is."

Penelope smiled at the mother, then asked Emily, "Did I do okay?"

"Yeah, so cool." Emily nodded with a wide smile.

Darryl stood flabbergasted. Penelope had drawn a cartoon of Emily and Tyson at the beach eating tacos. He'd never met anyone who surprised him so much. Or who he'd gotten so wrong. He always thought life was very much black and white, but these days proved that theory wrong. Penelope lived in the gray, and he happened to like that spot very much. She wasn't bringing him trouble like he thought, she was bringing him warm things that hit him straight in the chest; things he didn't even know he was missing, and that he didn't want to lose.

Emily and her mom started talking about the drawing, so Darryl stepped forward, nudging Penelope's shoulder, and gestured her out the door. He gave the mom a quick smile and mouthed, *We'll be right out here,* leaving them with Tyson loving all over the girl. When Penelope finally joined him in the hallway, he asked, "You draw?"

She shrugged. "I became a doodle expert in high school, since you know…I was terrible at school."

Darryl chuckled. "Luckily for Emily, that was the perfect skill to have today."

She snorted a laugh. "If I could only tell my dad now, then he wouldn't think that my entire education was wasted."

She sounded flippant, but Darryl assumed there was some truth in there too. "Maybe you should tell him what you've been doing with your time here."

"Maybe." She smiled.

Bullshit. He could sniff that lie out easily. She wasn't

going to tell her dad shit, and Darryl knew enough about her family that he imagined they wouldn't care anyway. They didn't even seem to *see* Penelope at all from what she'd told him.

"So," she said, changing the subject, "why are we out here?"

He allowed the shift and moved down the hallway to the chairs. "I always leave for a little while." He took a seat.

She dropped down next to him. "Why?"

"Because we're strangers to Emily and her mom." He crossed his arms, settling back into the cold, hard chair. "They'll be more guarded if we're in there with Tyson. And he's good for the kid. Good for the mom too."

Penelope watched him a moment then closed the distance and threw her arms around him so tight that it completely caught him off guard. It'd been so long since a woman offered affection. It didn't take him long to catch up and return the embrace. The aroma of her vanilla-scented shampoo filled his nostrils as he dropped his head into her neck. And when she leaned away, he didn't want her to let go. "What was that for?" he asked.

"Just giving you something *you* deserve." She stared into the room across from them and dropped her hand onto his thigh, awakening a part of him that shouldn't be stirring in *this* place. "It feels weird not bringing Christmas gifts or something." She turned to him, gaze concerned. "Shouldn't we have brought something?"

Darryl shook his head. "The mayor comes by on Christmas Day with gifts," he explained, taking her hand to bring her touch closer to his knee. "That's why I'm here to make sure we get those gifts right. Don't want any mistakes."

"Yeah, no kidding." She sat back and watched Emily and her mother through the window, laughing and doting on Ty, who ate up everything minute, his eyes bright, tongue wagging out the side of his mouth. "You wouldn't know, would you?"

Darryl glanced sideways. "Know what?"

"That Emily is sick," Penelope said softly, squeezing his fingers tight. "They look happy."

"I imagine they are happy," he said.

"I wonder how that can that be possible?" Penelope asked, eyebrows drawn tight.

Darryl drew in a long deep breath before addressing her. "From being a cop, I've learned there are good moments within the bad. I imagine the families here probably hang on to those good moments more than people who haven't experienced illness or tragedy."

Penelope's face suddenly become unreadable, but before he could check in on that, Tyson whined. That usually meant that Emily was getting tired or antsy, and Tyson knew it.

Darryl rose. "Time to move on."

He took a step forward when Penelope caught his hand, pulling him back. "Thank you."

"For?"

She stepped closer. Her eyes were watery. "For making me do this."

He cupped her face and closed the rest of the distance. "I think I had my own motivation for suggesting the community service, and we both know exactly what that was." More time together.

She nodded and smiled.

He tucked her hair behind her ear, loving the silkiness of the soft strands along with how she leaned into him. "That said," he added, "you bought out the bakery, you drew the picture. That's all you, I did none of that. Don't forget that."

She rose on her tiptoes and pressed a quick kiss to his lips. "Better stop all those compliments. I might get a big head." She strode away laughing and entered the room again.

He stared after her. No, she wouldn't. If only she did think more of herself, maybe she'd take a chance on something real.

THE HOSPITAL VISIT lasted the remainder of the day, and by the time Darryl dropped Penelope off at her cousins'

house, her hand hurt from all the drawings she'd done. Not that she cared; she would've done more if anyone needed her to. When they arrived home, Maisie insisted Darryl stay for dinner, and after a reassuring look from Penelope, he agreed. Which was how they ended up at the brewery.

The barn had been stained in a rich cherry color. The beams were left open, with the hay loft still there at the back of the barn, now holding empty kegs with the Three Chicks logo on the front. And beneath the hay loft were large refrigerators.

When they entered, Darryl had made a purely masculine sound that came from deep in his chest. The sound was one of total delight. He strode down the cement floors between the large brewing tanks, his hands stuffed in his pockets, as if he was afraid he'd dive in for a drink.

Penelope smiled, and after today, that felt good. Because even she was feeling things she couldn't quite put a finger on.

"A man could get thirsty in here," Darryl eventually said, turning around to her.

Penelope snorted a laugh. "I could get into a lot of trouble in here."

He reached for her, his smile a mix of heat and tenderness. "I'm beginning to enjoy the trouble you bring."

Sure, it was easy to hope he meant that, but the truth

was, Penelope liked a bit of trouble and there would be no apologizing for it. "That's only because I'm not here very long, and I'm on my best behavior."

"And why is that exactly?" he asked, taking her hand and turning around the corner to walk down the other aisle in the brewery. "Why is the wild girl who lives life on her terms, skating drunk on fountains, suddenly on her best behavior?"

"For my cousins."

He cocked his head and chuckled. "You do know that I'm trained in spotting a lie."

"Great." She rolled her eyes. "What are you now, a mind reader?"

He took hold of her chin, his eyes hardening. "Don't deflect."

"Well, that cop look is effective, I'll give you that," she said with a shake of her head to remove his hand.

"Why do you think I did it?" He grinned, shoving his hands back into his pockets. "But indulge me anyway. What's the *real* reason?"

She inhaled sharply and strode forward ahead of him now, not really sure how much she wanted to tell him. "I'm just trying to hit the nice list this year, that's all." She looked over her shoulder, and Darryl studied her carefully. Too carefully, in fact. She glanced ahead of her again and shrugged a little. "Besides, I know my cousins think I'm this big drinker because I work as a bartender.

Maybe I used to be, but that's not really me anymore. I want them to see me for...*me*."

"Then what happened at the fountain?" he called out behind her.

Her throat tightened. He suddenly had her hand in his and tugged him into her. His warm gaze met hers, and it was impossible not to answer him. "It was just this place. It's so...friendly and Christmas-y...and family-oriented." She paused. Then forced the words out. "The first few days here were hard. I felt outside of everything. Apart from everyone. It had all gotten to be too much. It's better now, though."

"Ah, I see," he said, with no judgment in his eyes.

He kept her hand in his as they headed back down the aisle toward the double barn doors, with the tasting room off to the left.

Just as she reached for the door, he stopped her, turning her into all his warmth and strength. "For what it's worth, I'm proud of you for not only yesterday but today too."

Her eyes stung. "Geez, they should just call this town, River Rock, the place where people are so nice they make you want to cry."

He barked a loud laugh then dipped his chin. "Or maybe River Rock, the place where you finally hear the things you should've always heard." He didn't wait for an answer; instead, he kissed her, a warm and sweet kiss that made her fingers and toes and other parts of her tingle.

When he broke the kiss, he opened the door, leading her outside into the brisk chilly night air.

The moment they went out the door, a snowball flew toward them and hit Darryl in the thigh.

"Ha. Ha. Got you," Mason squealed.

"Oh, it's so on," Darryl said, dropping Penelope's hand to chase after a now screaming Mason.

Penelope laughed, tucking her hands into her coat pockets then making her way back into the house. She hung her coat on the hook then ventured into the living room and stared out the window, watching Darryl toss a tiny snowball Mason's way which hit him in the boot. He laughed then threw another snowball Darryl's way. The kid had an arm.

"You okay?"

Penelope sighed and glanced over her shoulder, finding Maisie behind her. "Yes. No." She shook her head. "I don't know, to be honest."

Maisie gave a pouty look then sidled in next to her, wrapping an arm around Penelope. "Tomorrow is Christmas Eve. No one should look as tangled up as you do right now."

Yeah, tangled up, that explained it. "We went to the hospital today. Darryl's dog picked up all the kids' letters to Santa there."

"Ugh." Maisie's arm tightened. "Well, that's heart-wrenching."

"Incredibly." Penelope dropped her head against Maisie's, staring off at the snow fluttering down from the evergreen tree. "More than anything, being there made me feel like an asshole."

"An asshole?"

Penelope waited for the lump in her throat to ease up before she explained, "I've got this whole life where all I do is run from one place to the next. I'm not doing anything that matters. And here are all these little kids that would give anything for a week, another day. Hell, maybe even another hour." Her voice cracked, emotion she'd been fighting flooding her. She quickly wiped away a tear. "So, yeah, I felt like an asshole who had the only thing anyone in that hospital wanted—more time."

Maisie hugged Penelope's arm, squeezing tight. "I can't imagine any of that was easy today, but I'm sure that big lug Tyson made the kiddies smile."

"A lot, actually," Penelope said, spotting Darryl running across the yard then tucking himself behind one of the trees, a smile on his face. Penelope couldn't help but wonder if some of this was to shake what he saw today too. "Darryl's a real sweetheart, isn't he?"

Maisie sighed, stepping away to sit on the window frame. "Yeah, he changed a little after his divorce, but honestly, I think it was for the better. He seems to have come out of his shell more; he does more for the community and stuff now."

Penelope kinda got that. Hell, she'd been buying treats and drawing pictures, and she knew why. She was trying to prove to herself she was better than her parents made her out to be, maybe she just didn't want to admit that. Now thinking it over, she began to wonder if Darryl's motivation sat somewhere between trying to put on a good face after the pain of a failed marriage and proving to himself that he was nothing like his deadbeat dad.

Mason suddenly found Darryl, and Darryl lurched forward, picking up the boy and slinging him over his shoulder, sending Mason smiling from ear-to-ear. "Well, he's definitely the nicest guy I've ever met," Penelope stated.

"Me too," Maisie said. "He's definitely one of the good ones. I tried to hook up Clara with him."

Penelope turned her head to the side so fast, it felt like it almost spun around. "You did?"

"Yes," Clara said, entering the living room carrying a brown paper grocery bag. "And I said no."

Maisie rolled her eyes, following her sister into the kitchen.

When Penelope joined them, Maisie was already scooping the first thing out of the bag to help Clara put away the groceries. "Only because Darryl was best friends with the-guy-who-shall-not-be-named," Maisie said. "Which was a million years ago." She placed the block of butter into the fridge. "All I'm saying is that it's a shame a man like Darryl is single."

Penelope looked away, quickly avoiding that conversation, and grabbed the veggies off the counter to stuff in the veggie drawer.

"I quit."

Every set of eyes turned onto Amelia. Three things happened simultaneously. Maisie burst out laughing. Clara plugged her nose. Penelope bit her lip to not be like Maisie.

"Please tell me that is not what I think it is," Clara muttered.

"Barf?" Amelia asked, her chest soaking wet with bits of things Penelope didn't want to identify. "Yes, that's exactly what it is," Amelia snapped. "I was helping a group get their drunk-ass friend on the bus after the last tour, and he decided I was a better place to puke on then…I don't know…the ground."

Penelope bit her lip harder.

"Wow," Maisie said seriously. "That blows chunks."

Clara laughed.

Amelia's eyes narrowed into slits. "Not funny in the least."

Maisie lifted her fingers. "Maybe just a little?"

"No, not even the tiniest amount." Amelia glared at

Clara. "I'm not joking. I quit. Someone else can do the tours." Without waiting for a reply, she left the kitchen.

"Poor Amelia," Penelope said.

"Oh, please," Clara said, scrunching the paper bag in her hands. "I have cleaned up her barf at least five times over the years. This is just payback."

Maisie giggled. "I better go check on her." She scooted out of the kitchen, and soon her footsteps could be heard thundering up the staircase.

Penelope grabbed the bananas off the counter and hung them on the fruit basket, when Clara broke the silence. "You seem to have a way with drunk people and entertainment, maybe the tours could be your thing if you stick around."

Penelope's mouth fell open before she sputtered, "I'm not...who said...I don't know why..."

Clara gave an easy smile and sidled up next to her, staring out at Darryl, who currently was getting a snowball in the gut. "You were ripped away from here before. That wasn't your choice. But that's changed now, hasn't it?"

Penelope searched for words, anything to try and declare that staying was the worst idea ever.

But the words never came.

Clara laughed softly, obviously liking Penelope speechlessness, before she strode away.

"Didn't you say that I had to make sure Christmas

wasn't full of drama this year?" Penelope called after her.

"When have you ever listened to me?" Clara countered.

CHAPTER EIGHT

DARKNESS FADED AWAY to light as Penelope peeled open her eyes. It took her a moment to remember that she and Darryl had returned to Darryl's place after dinner with her cousins. She'd come to love the family dinners they did together. She recalled the two glasses of wine she ingested that apparently had given her enough liquid courage to rip Darryl's clothes off the second they entered his house, and she'd very much remembered how he tasted when she took him into her mouth. Which lasted until he began trembling then pressed her up against the wall and gave her a mind-blowing orgasm.

That all was perfectly fine.

What wasn't okay was the warm and heavy weight pressing against her chest. Any bit of sleepy haze faded in a millisecond. "Darryl," she whispered, frightened to move.

He lay motionless next to her, snoring softly, with his back to her.

The problem was, Darryl wasn't the only one snoring. Ebenezer was curled up on her chest, the soft snores of the big tomcat breaking into the silence. "Darryl," she said a little bit louder, scared if she made a move, her face would become a cat scratching post. "Darryl," she said louder.

From a dead sleep, Darryl shot up in the bed. "What's wrong?"

"Help me," she barely managed.

Darryl flicked on the bedside light, stared at her face, then the cat, and began laughing.

"This is *not* funny," Penelope said seriously. "He's going to kill me."

"I've never seen him do this with anyone but Tyson." Darryl rubbed his eyes, sitting up a little, then when he dropped his hands, his grin appeared. "He likes you."

"He doesn't like anyone," she countered. "You named him Ebenezer, remember? He's just warming me up to eat me."

Darryl's mouth curved. He settled back against the pillow and stared at them both a moment. "I'm not exactly sure how to handle this."

"You're a cop," Penelope grumbled. "Surely, you can handle a cat. Get him off me."

Darryl chuckled and winked. "Just kidding. I wanted to enjoy the view a little longer." He clapped.

Ebenezer opened his eyes, yawned and stood up, but then those sharp eyes came to Penelope's. He stared at her, looking as horrified as she was, or maybe that was just the way his brow looked. Certainly this was up for debate.

"Don't kill me," Penelope whispered. "I taste terrible."

Darryl scoffed. "Wrong. You taste incredible."

Ebenezer jumped off the bed.

"You can breathe now," Darryl said, flicking off the light again. "He doesn't like being caught loving on anyone or anything." Darryl gathered her in his arms until he was spooning her side, while she lay on her back, his leg draped over hers. "See? All safe." Tyson came up to the bed, and Darryl gave him a head scratch. "Nothing to worry about, bud. Back to bed."

Tyson yawned and then curled up beside the bed on the floor.

Penelope did not move, her heart hammering in her ears.

Silence drifted between them for a few minutes before Darryl's chuckle filled the dark room. "Sleeping happens when you shut your eyes."

"How can you tell I'm not sleeping?"

"Are you sleeping?"

"No."

"Then that's how I know."

She laughed softly then turned into him, his breath brushing across her cheek. "I think my flight mode has been activated."

"Just settle," he said, his voice low and smooth.

"Says the guy that didn't have a killer cat sleeping on his chest."

Darryl moved away then flicked on the light again. When he faced her, his playful expression she thought she'd find was nowhere in sight. Hardness lay in his every line. "All right, if you don't want to sleep, let's talk." He took a deep breath. "Stay."

She blinked, thinking she heard him wrong.

Then she realized she hadn't, as he added, "I know this is going to rock the boat. That maybe what you want is a world away from here, but I couldn't live with myself if I don't say it. I don't want you to leave after Christmas, Penelope. Stay here, with me. Let's give this a shot."

Her heart promptly landed in her stomach. "It's more complicated than my just staying."

"Why? It seems pretty simple to me. Don't leave. All fixed."

"What about my job?"

"There are bartending jobs here. Or you could find a new one."

"Where would I live?"

"I have no doubt your cousins would take you in until you got settled."

She was beginning to run out of reasons not to, and by the intensity in his gaze, he seemed like he knew it too.

"There's your new adventure," he said, sliding his knuckles across her cheek. "Do something you've never done. Stick."

Her throat tightened, skin flushed *hot,* and she shifted against the mattress, suddenly realizing that having Ebenezer on her seemed easy in comparison to this conversation. "I can't—"

Darryl pressed his finger against her mouth. "Just think about it, that's all I'm asking." He slowly removed his finger, and in its place came his mouth.

And damn was it a fine mouth.

He swept her away with his kiss, and she became mindless to him, losing herself in the passion he invoked.

"Now, how about we get you settled for the night?" he said, moving atop her until they were pressed together flesh against flesh.

She slid her hands up his warm back, letting her fingers explore the lines of each groove of his incredible body. She slid that touch lower over his fine muscular ass, liking how when she touched him there, his breath became a little rougher.

"Damn, sugar. You make me want to bring out my naughty side," he said roughly, then broke away to reach into the drawer.

She expected him to pull out a condom. Instead, he slowly pulled out a camouflage bandana. The side of his mouth curved up, probably at her growing curiosity.

Naked and hard, he knelt between her thighs and began folding, until she understood.

A blindfold.

He lifted his warm eyes to hers. "Any problem with this?"

Her nipples tightened and heat warmed low in her belly. "Well, this is a first for me. And for what it's worth, I am a big fan of the naughty side of you."

He chucked, low and deep. "I'll take that as consent." Something intense and hot flashed in his eyes.

As he placed the blindfold over her eyes, she realized the flash was determination. Maybe determination to show her that there was no better place to be than right there with him.

The thought was hastily ripped from her as he began kissing his way down her neck until he had her breasts in his hands. He squeezed them together, licking a nipple before licking the other, sucking on them, nibbling until she squirmed in need for him to move lower. And she couldn't quite remember the reasons she'd ever want to leave him.

"I'll take care of you tonight, Penelope," he murmured.

Her heart raced again, but this time, the spike came from a place of vulnerability. A place she'd never felt before. Maybe that was Darryl's thing, he knew how to bare a woman's soul to him, but she felt her control slipping away, until her fingers fisted in the sheets as his tongue slid across her clit. Her hands came down onto his head.

"Ah-ah, not your game, sugar." He grasped her hips and flipped her over, until her head lay against the pillow and he brought her ass high. Her nudged her legs open, and she felt the heat rise to her face as she lay there as exposed as she possibly could be.

He squeezed her bottom, spreading her cheeks, obviously examining. His fingers dug in with his groan that came from deep in his chest, telling her he liked what he saw. Then he reached for her arms and held both her wrists in one hand on top of her back. Without missing a beat, she shivered against his soft wet tongue as he slowly licked her folds. She shamelessly arched her back, showing him where she wanted him to go. And he went there, flicking his tongue back down her sex until he reached her clit. Gripping her wrists tight, he didn't tease, didn't play around. No, Darryl had learned her *on* spots already, and he used that knowledge to get her to the exact place he wanted.

Screaming his name.

He took her there and beyond. She shuddered against his mouth, flying on a high she never wanted to come down from. A high she thought would never end.

And it didn't end.

Darryl entered her before she came down. He wasn't gentle. Maybe he'd been teased too much. But he gave a few slow strokes to warm her up and allow her wetness to soak over the condom, and then he unleashed himself.

She squeezed her eyes shut beneath the blindfold, not even sure the orgasm before this one faded. Pleasure stole over every thought. Sensation flooded every molecule of her being. He gripped her wrists, pinning her, and she didn't want him to let go. For all the moments she felt she had no one, his tight hold eased those painful spots on her soul.

"All mine tonight," Darryl growled, sounding both possessive and aroused.

He slapped her bottom, and she gasped with the way heat flooded her. Her legs began trembling when he reached around and rubbed her clit with his fingers. Beneath the blindfold, she let the sensation overtake her, trusting him to bring her out of her mind.

She went to places she'd never gone before. She felt the hard shudders of her body and heard him roaring his climax, but she tumbled back into the darkness, pulsating with a beautiful pleasure, vaguely aware that while what was between her and Darryl was complicated, it somehow, was also the easiest thing she'd ever done. Ten years ago, she'd been captivated by him. That hadn't changed. And being there, in the warmth of Darryl's arms as he gathered her close, felt right.

The safest and scariest place she'd ever been in her life.

CHAPTER NINE

EDISON LIGHTS HUNG from the rafters of the old barn that had been converted into a banquet hall a few years back. Darryl grabbed the Santa coat out of his duffel bag. Tonight, his job was to hand out gifts spontaneously, as the event planners took care of all the things that Darryl knew nothing about. Like, decorating and party food.

Out of sight behind one of the large beams, he removed his button-down and T-shirt, then slid into the Santa coat. The coat and pants were thick and hot, and the Santa hat didn't help much either. After he buttoned the coat up, he strode around the large beam, pleased by the number of people spilling through the doors. Months, he'd been planning the main event, alongside the event planners. Things had come together nicely.

He reached for his bag of gifts donated by some of the locals, when he heard the captain say, "You better be treating that girl right. She's made you look like damn Santa Claus."

Darryl straightened, finding his captain casually

dressed, with a beer in his hand.

The captain smiled, leaning against the wooden beam, and added, "The mayor called this morning to inform me she's been hearing about how you and Penelope have really outdone yourselves during these events and went beyond what anyone expected of either of you." The captain cupped his shoulder, pride beaming in his eyes. "Done good, Wilson. Done good."

"Thank you, sir." Warmth carried through Darryl. Not having a father figure in his life had been a blow. The captain filled that void at times. Which had been another reason Darryl's drunk screw-up after his divorce had been such a shitshow. Darryl hadn't only disappointed himself. He'd also disappointed the man he looked up to. "But believe me when I tell you, all those extras were from Penelope." And *that* was still the best surprise of all. He'd always wondered what the draw to Penelope had been back in the day. Now he knew it wasn't only the intensity between them, but she was also a good person.

The captain's fingers tightened around Darryl's shoulder again. "Ah, perhaps that's true enough, but you were the one who suggested the community service in the first place." The captain lifted his beer in salute then strode toward his wife on the other side of the barn.

People were still coming through the doors, while the band who also worked at Kinky Spurs, the best watering hole in town, played the fourth song of the night. Soon the party would be happening, and once Darryl got his Santa work completed, he'd spend the rest of the night with the only woman on his mind.

She still hadn't answered his question from last night.

He wanted that answer.

Darryl reached for the bag of gifts again, when a softer, sexier voice said behind him, "Hi, Santa. Am I on the nice list this year?"

He turned and immediately reached for Penelope's hand. Damn. His body heated and hardened in a single breath. "I'm beginning to think it would serve me better if you were on the naughty list." He pulled her in close and kissed her, not caring who saw him, only caring that his lips met hers. "My. My," he said when he backed away. He held her hand and twirled his finger, and she obliged, giving him a little spin. She wore green-and-red stripe leggings with a little green dress, and sleek, sexy black heels that did incredible things for her legs. Her hair was in big curls and her makeup was darker than he'd seen it. He thought maybe he should just skip the *work* part all together.

The song shifted to a slow song. "Come on," he said, taking her hand, leading her onto the dance floor. "We've got work, but first, let's dance." He pulled her in close, loving how she smiled sweetly at him.

A dozen or more people danced around them, but he

was focused on *her*. On the way she stared into his eyes and felt all soft against him. He didn't want her to leave. And he hoped she realized she didn't want to either.

"Stop taking up all the room, Wilson."

Darryl snorted, recognizing the voice. He turned to Nash Blackshaw who danced with his wife, Megan, in his arms. "Aren't you the one who usually takes up most the room, Blackshaw?"

Nash barked a loud laugh.

Darryl glanced at Megan. "Thank you for providing the band again."

"Thank the band." Megan smiled; her unique eyes, one blue, the other brown, were bright tonight. "They're doing all the work. Since we're kidless tonight, I'm just here for the dancing and booze." She laughed as Nash twirled her away.

In their place, Darryl noticed the other two Blackshaw brothers, Shep and Chase, along with their wives, Emma and Harper. Their family had suffered a blow after losing their father, then some financial and personal trouble came their way when they developed a new guest ranch, but anytime Darryl saw them now, they all seemed happy and busy with their kids.

"They're all brothers, aren't they?"

Darryl glanced at Penelope, finding her watching the group. "Yeah, good people too."

She tipped her head to the side and gave him a

knowing look. "Isn't everyone here good people?"

"Most yes, but not all." He paused then explained, "Being a cop means seeing the worst in the people sometimes. And the worst can, at times, be dark."

"I suppose that's probably very true." She dropped her head onto his shoulder and sank deeper into his hold, letting him guide the way through the dance as Dalton, the lead singer of the Kinky Spurs band sang his heart out like he was putting on a big show in a stadium. The man could sing. There was a story there. Dalton could've been famous and was nearly signed, but his sick mother kept him at home.

Darryl felt for the guy, hoping something good came to Dalton soon. He turned his attention back to Penelope and dropped his head into her neck, giving her a soft kiss there.

"If I ask you something, will you tell me the truth?" she asked a moment later.

He met those pretty eyes again. "That's all I know how to do."

"Do you do all this community service during the holidays because it keeps you from being alone?"

He pressed his lips to the top of her head. "Who's the mind reader now?"

"I learned from the very best."

"I'll take that compliment and wear it proudly," he said, leaning back to meet her gaze, and then he dug into that place he wasn't very fond of going. "To answer your question, yes, I like doing things for others during Christmas. I didn't volunteer as much when I was married because Natalie didn't like to be in the public that way, but my mother loved volunteering. It's a good way to honor her every year. Of course, this year is a little different. All these events are new, and I'm heading them up for a purely selfish reason too."

"Which is?"

"To look better for a possible promotion."

She studied him a moment. "Nothing wrong with trying to further yourself."

He gave her a little kiss for that. He dropped his head into Penelope's neck again, liking being right *there*, drawing in her sugary aroma.

Tomorrow she'd have Christmas with her cousins and then she'd be leaving the next day. He'd done the laidback thing with Natalie, trying to make her happy, even though he knew it was hard. He couldn't be that guy anymore. And feeling like this thing with Penelope was the best thing that happened to him in years, he asked, "Have you put any thought into what we talked about last night?"

Her eyes softened, as did her voice. "Darryl, it's just…"

"Complicated," he said, pulling her soft curves against him tighter.

He felt the clamminess of her palm against his. "I really like you and this…but I'm not this girl."

He matched the rhythm of the song, swaying his hips to the beat, watching her carefully, trying to understand. "What's that? The girl who's got people who care about her? The girl who's doing great things for others? The girl who's happy with me?" He tried to take the sharpness out of his voice and failed.

"I like traveling, being free."

Bullshit. That was a cop-out, and they both knew it. "Maybe it's time to do something you wouldn't normally do." He dropped his mouth to hers, knowing this wouldn't be an easy decision. They had five days together. How could he even dare ask her to uproot her life for him? "I know this is hard. I know what I'm asking is a little bit out there."

Her brows rose. "A little bit?"

He chuckled, brushing his lips across hers. "Okay, a lot a bit," he whispered against her mouth before leaning way. "But it doesn't change the fact that I don't want you to go. Your spontaneity has made me realize there is value in that. I want to be 'out there' too. With you. I see you. All of *you*. We got a second chance at this again. I refuse to waste it." He noted the tightness rising in her expression. "We have tonight, and I'll enjoy it, but here's an idea: If you decide to stay, at midnight, meet me under the mistletoe. If you're not there, then I'll know tonight is all we've got, and I'll respect that."

"Just like that?" She looked doubtful.

He gave a firm nod. "Just like that." Because he wouldn't be on the list of people who didn't support and trust her to make her own choices. Not today. Not tomorrow. Not ever.

AN HOUR LATER, with Darryl handing out another round of gifts, Penelope headed outside. Whoever made this velvet dress wasn't thinking comfort. She needed cool air in a big bad way. Just out in front of the double doors, she pulled down her long winter jacket over her butt and dropped onto one of the hay bales set outside for decoration that only had a sprinkling of snow covering the top. She slipped her aching feet out of her heels, the brisk wind brushing against her toes. The band belted out a Jason Aldean song back inside, and she heard the crowd cheering. She'd danced, given out gifts, and laughed so damn much, she couldn't recall every having such a good night when she hadn't had some liquid happiness to help her along.

The snow fluttered down in big snowflakes from the dark cloudy sky. She held out her hand, and a chilly snowflake landed on her palm before melting away. Tonight was perfect in every which way, but as much as

River Rock had been a replacement for a normal Christmas with her family, it wasn't her mom and dad, and as much as she'd been trying not to think about it, she was wishing they were here too.

It occurred to her that maybe it was time for her to be the better person. She reached for the cell phone that was tucked into the pocket of her elf dress from the costume store. She found her mom's name in her contacts then dialed the number.

"Hello."

Penelope cringed at the high-pitched sound of her stepsister's voice. She was five years younger and didn't know the meaning of hard work. "Hey, Lizzy, can I talk with my mom?"

The phone dropped on something hard.

A beat later, there was shuffling on the line, then Mom said, "Hi, Penelope, how are things?"

"Good," Penelope said, shifting back against the hay bale until her aching feet were dangling. "I'm in River—"

"Yes, Eric," Mom said. "Yes, that one. Sorry, what was that, Penelope?"

"I'm in—"

"I'll be the hat, Brandon," Mom interjected. "Sorry, Penelope, we're playing Monopoly. Things are good, then?"

Penelope's chest squeezed. All the things she'd hope to say, wanted to say, suddenly faded away. "Yeah, things are good. Just calling to say Merry Christmas."

Don't hang up. Say something. "Same to you, Penelope." A pause. "Best I go now, everyone is ready to play and they're waiting for me."

"Bye." Penelope forced her voice through her tight throat.

"By—" The line went dead before she could even finish.

Penelope dropped her head, staring down at her cell phone. She inhaled and exhaled deeply, keeping it together, her breath a thick fog in front of her. Okay, so that sucked. Maybe her mom was just busy. That did happen. Penelope gave her head a little shake, blowing off the sting of rejection. She could handle this. Darryl was a total put-together guy that didn't seem to let his deadbeat dad shake his confidence. She found her father's contact information then hit dial.

He answered on the third ring. "Penelope, what's wrong?"

"Nothing," she said, putting as much Christmas cheer into her voice that she could possibly find. "I'm calling to wish you a Merry Christmas."

"Oh, Merry Christmas to you too." He hesitated, clearing his throat. "The accountant called and said you spent some money. Did you buy yourself an early Christmas gift?"

Of course, he went straight to money. That was

typically all he ever talked about, and most of the conversation was his demanding that she use what he gave her. "Something like that."

"Well, that's what it's there for." Another heavier pause.

But in that pause, she heard the laughter and voices in her father's family home. Part of her wanted to ask, *Why did you lie about traveling? Why don't you want me with you?* The other part of her refused to go there.

"Now don't spend it stupidly, Penelope," her father added with his firm CEO voice. "I hope you're being smart about things."

Come home. Come here. Be with us. We want you here.

All the things she hoped he'd say never came. Darryl had found a way to be the bigger man. To prove his deadbeat dad couldn't impact his life. She wasn't nearly that strong. The rejection stung, opening old wounds that could never heal. "I—"

"You what?"

More laughter. More celebrations, all of which didn't include her. And she didn't know why. She never knew why. "Nothing. Just…Merry Christmas."

"To you as well."

She caught a voice in the background before her dad said, "Listen, gotta go, kid. Talk soon."

The phone line went dead. Yeah, she was an adult, not needing her parents as much, but she still needed them a little, something they seemed to forget. She stared down at the blank screen, her eyes stinging. Maybe she'd had blinders on lately. Hell, maybe it was Christmas cheer that got in the way. For four days, she had tasted what life would have been like had her parents never dragged her away, went through a brutal divorce, and then got themselves a new family to love. For four days, she forgot that emptiness that lived deep in her chest, the hole that never seemed healable. For four days, she remembered who she'd once been when she was seventeen years old and kissed a cute boy.

But that wasn't real life.

And there was a reason she didn't go to these warm places in her heart. Because those warm places lied and hurt.

"Hey, it's the girl from the fountain."

Penelope jerked her head up, finding a group of six people standing around her. She didn't recognize any of them. The girl who showed up to River Rock would've jumped up and laughed her way through her embarrassment, but that seemed impossible to do now. "Yep, that's me." *The woman who's nothing but trouble, a hassle to anyone she cares about.*

"You were so awesome that night," the pretty blonde said, wrapping her arm into the guy standing next to her.

They looked around Penelope's age, maybe a little young. "Thanks. I have a special talent when it comes to skating in high heels."

The group laughed.

"Up for some more fun?" another one of the guys said, staring at Penelope like she was on the menu tonight. *His menu.* "We're going to get some drinking in here, then heading over to Kinky Spurs."

Kinky Spurs—the bar where she'd gotten in trouble, where all this began.

The emptiness in her chest split wide open, a heaviness sinking in deep into her bones. She wasn't this woman Darryl made her believe she could be. And maybe it was time they both realized that. "I doubt I'll leave with you," she said, pushing off the hay bale, sliding back into her high heels. "But the drinks sound like exactly what I need."

DARRYL FINISHED HANDING out the final gift then set the Santa bag onto the table next to him. The party was in full swing. Everyone looked to be having fun, dancing and drinking, and celebrating Christmas in grand style. It occurred to Darryl that for all the trouble he thought Penelope was going to be for him, it turned out, she put him in a better light with his bosses than he could have put himself in. He'd always played things safe, but damn if he didn't like stirring things up these past couple days with her.

He liked this life. Going back to a world without Penelope in it didn't appeal in the least. Now he simply needed to get her to see that her place was here, with *him*.

"Darryl."

Someone had yelled his name over the music. He glanced through the crowd, and when he heard his name called a second time, he spotted Maisie pushing her way through the people and waving at him.

He met her halfway.

"You have to help me before something really bad happens," she said when she reached him.

"Of course," he said. "What do you need?"

She grabbed the sleeve of his Santa suit and weaved him through the dancefloor full of people. Someone pinched him on the ass and said something about a *Naughty Santa*, but Darryl stayed focused on Maisie as she led him toward the bar. When he got there, he understood the problem immediately.

Penelope was dancing on the bar in a suggestive manner to a rowdy group of men cheering her on. Darryl took note of the mayor watching her who clapped along, obviously enjoying her dance, and his captain, who was clearly too in love with her now to see anything but how good she'd been to the people in their town. Darryl turned back to Penelope and sighed as he watched a mirror image of her dance on the fountain that first night he saw her again. Only this time, Amelia was also there yelling at her to get down. "What happened?" he asked Maisie. "The last time I saw Penelope, she was fine."

Maisie shrugged. "I have no idea, but by the looks of this, something bad."

Yeah, Darryl agreed. Because now he knew when this wild side of Penelope came out, it was because she was hurting. The past four days with her had told him that. And for once, the cop didn't come out when he stared at her, the man did, and seeing her break apart made him want to hurt whatever or whoever was hurting her.

"Clara is out in the car waiting for us," Maisie said, bringing Darryl's attention back to her. "Help. Please. Before she does something she can't take back."

Darryl doubted anything she did could ruin the town's perception of her now. He nodded anyway then approached the men, not blind to the jealous heat that rushed through his veins at the way they gawked at her. "Move along," he told the men firmly, who were regulars on the bar scene. "Now." He tried to erase the bite in his voice and failed miserably.

Each man frowned his way before heading back onto the dance floor.

Darryl pushed a stool out of the way then got closer to the bar and slowly glanced up. "Penelope."

"Oooh, there's my sexy Santa," she practically

purred, hands in the air, dancing her heart out.

Damn she was beautiful.

She waggled her eyebrows at him. "Why don't you hop up here and we'll give 'em a real good Christmas show."

"Penelope," he said softer now. Before when he saw her this way at the fountain, he thought she was reckless and wild and pure *trouble*. Now…well, now he saw her heart bleeding in her glossy eyes. And that was the endgame for him. That pain, he wanted it *gone.* Plus, from the glossiness of her eyes, he suspected whatever shots she'd downed had only begun to hit her. "It's time to come down now, sugar."

She rolled her hips. "You wanna go down on me?"

Yeah, most times, he did.

But this was taking a downward direction. Fast. Before this went from fun and games to something embarrassing, he grabbed her around the legs until he had her over his shoulder. The crowd cheered her on as Penelope burst out laughing. To keep everything light, Darryl turned to crowd, purposely glancing in the mayor's and the captain's direction. "This elf is calling it a night. She apparently helped with the cause a little too much."

The captain smiled. The mayor laughed. The bullet had been dodged.

Darryl followed Maisie and Amelia out to where

Clara was waiting outside the car, her arms crossed, her lips in a thin line. "Give me a minute, all right?" he asked her cousins.

Clara frowned at Penelope then nodded at Darryl. "Yeah, all right." She moved behind him to join her sisters.

Darryl slowly lowered a laughing Penelope down, then helped her into the back seat of the car. He squatted next to the open door and waited for her to acknowledge him there. She finally did and turned her head, her eyes beaming. "Are you planning on tucking me into bed too, Santa?" she asked playfully. "Want me to be a bad girl this Christmas?"

Did he ever.

Also, not the right time to indulge those thoughts.

He tucked her hair behind her ear, staring into the sweetness of her soul. For all the time he desperately worried about his promotion and making sure everything was perfect, he realized that none of it really mattered when Penelope was sad. "What happened tonight?" he asked.

"I danced." She smiled. "And…maybe…had a shot or two."

She'd run from this conversation. He knew she wanted to. She'd proven good at dodging things that left her exposed. For some reason, he couldn't let her do that anymore. He took her chin, capturing her gaze. "What happened that made you take that first shot?"

She jerked her chin away.

"Penelope." He waited for a moment then gently turned her chin back to him, not letting her run. Not anymore. "What happened?"

Her eyes welled and her chin quivered. "I called home."

Those three words told him everything he needed to know. The pain was written all over her face. The rejection. The loneliness. Something terrible had happened on the phone call, and he didn't doubt that *something* had to do with her shitty parents. "Penelope," he said softly. "Talk to me. Please."

"I can't." She shut her eyes, but not before a tear escaped down her cheek. "I don't want to think about this. I just want to go back to my cousins' house."

That he understood. He'd dealt with rejection for years as a kid when his father came back. And the loneliness when his mother passed away and his father still never made contact. Until Darryl realized he was better without him. Sometimes the pain was too hard to deal with, especially when you couldn't control how others acted. Sometimes you just had to deal with the shit that life threw at you the best you knew how. And that's what she had been doing for the last ten years— surviving. But Darryl knew a better way.

Before he could show her that way, she needed to be

sober.

He rose and then kissed her forehead. "Tomorrow, we'll talk. Tonight, just sleep." She kept her eyes shut tight as he closed the door.

Clara and Amelia got into the car, but Maisie hugged Darryl. "Don't give up on her." She leaned away and held onto his shoulders tight. "Promise me."

The promise was easy. "You have my word, Maisie. The very last thing I'd do is walk away from her."

Now he only needed to convince Penelope to commit in the same way.

CHAPTER TEN

ON CHRISTMAS MORNING, Darryl felt moody and tired. The plan on his day off was to drive up to the summit and spend the day hiking with Tyson. He needed air to clear his head, trying to figure out his next steps. Last night, he had planned to kiss Penelope under the mistletoe at midnight and make things solid between them.

This wasn't how he intended to spend Christmas morning.

The worst part was, he had no idea how to fix any of it. He didn't know the right thing to say to make the rejection with her parents sting less. And he knew he had to get that right. One mistake on his part, and she'd bolt, and he wouldn't blame her one bit. He also had no idea how to get her to stay. He needed a plan, and he hoped on his hike he'd find it.

"Come on, Ty," he said after opening the door to his cruiser. The dog jumped in, and Darryl shut the door, only for Tyson to stick his head out the open window and give Darryl's hand a lick.

Yeah, his mood with shit.

"I'm all right, bud," Darryl said, giving the pup a well-deserved head scratch.

"You promised me you wouldn't give up on Penelope."

Darryl glanced sideways, finding Maisie, her hands on her hips. "I didn't give up on her."

She stepped forward, slipped a little on the ice, then placed her hand on the cruiser and frowned. "You must have, because she's gone, so what did you do?"

This had to be some cruel joke. "What did *I* do?" he asked, flabbergasted.

"Yes. What. Did. You. Do?" Maisie tapped a furry boot against the snow-covered driveway. "Penelope changed her flight to earlier this morning and left in a big giant mess of emotions. She *never* gets like that, so you had to have done something to upset her."

Darryl turned to fully face Maisie now, shoving his hands into his pockets. He had to give it to Maisie. Most people balked at authority. She didn't even bat an eye. "I'm sorry to break it to you, but I haven't heard from Penelope since I put her in Clara's car last night. I planned to go see her after a hike."

Maisie's eyes narrowed into slits. "Is that the truth?"

"Yes," he defended, not blind to how sharp his voice became. "Jesus, Maisie. I asked Penelope to stay here, with me."

Maisie's expression pinched. "Hmm…" She nibbled her lip, watching Darryl closely, obviously having more to say.

Darryl waved her on. "You haven't held back yet. Why start now? What is it?" The Carter sisters weren't known for being particularly quiet about how they felt.

Maisie's expression softened as she moved closer to pet Tyson who still had his head resting on the open window. "Okay, so I'm about to do something I would never do." She hesitated, giving Tyson a quick kiss on the head. "Actually, I'm going to do two things, if we're getting down to the nitty-gritty."

"Maisie," Darryl said, urging her on.

She glanced up, moving away from Ty. "Get on with it, right?" At his nod, she said, "Number one, I don't share private conversations."

He hesitated, waiting for her to continue. When she didn't, he said, "All right, I understand."

"And you know that I'm only doing this because I think it's really important, and usually I'm a vault, all locked up tight."

Understanding what she needed from him, he said, "You're a good person, Maisie. I know this."

"Let's hope Penelope still thinks so after this." She sighed, folding her arms, leaning a shoulder against the cruiser. "So last night when I was putting Penelope's drunk ass to bed, she started sobbing, like really sad crying that comes from the gut, you know? When a heart bleeds and just won't quit."

"Yes, and…?"

"I guess Penelope called both her parents last night." Maisie's eyes saddened, and her voice softened. "They didn't even want to talk to her."

Darryl's chest tightened. He wasn't surprised. She'd mentioned calling home. "I'm sorry to say it, Maisie, but your aunt and uncle are assholes."

"Don't be sorry, you're right. They're a bunch of dicks," Maisie agreed with a firm nod. "Our family has been estranged from them for years, but the thing is, when she was talking, she also mentioned you. That you were just playing bad with her this week, but she's not someone that you could really want. That you deserve better than her. And that just made her sad."

His gut twisted and his hands fisted in his pockets. "I wish she'd told me that herself." Then he could've done something about it.

Maisie gave a long knowing look. "Yeah, well, would *you* speak about feelings if you were her?"

He didn't even have to think about it. "No, I wouldn't." How could she? The people who should listen to her, didn't. "All right, and what's the second thing that you'd never do?"

She reached into her back pocket, and her boot crunched against the snow on the driveway as she handed him an envelope. "This morning when I realized she had left, I found this in the garbage bin by her bed."

Darryl Wilson and his old address were written on the front. He'd been through enough investigations to know the ink was old. And that told him in his hands he had the letter that she'd told him she'd written when she was seventeen. "It's opened."

Maisie's shoulders curled and cheeks blushed. "Don't look at me like that. I feel bad enough about it, but something compelled me to open it, and then I knew I had to bring it to you." She couldn't even look him in the eyes. "Okay, so I've done my part. Bye." She turned to hurry away.

Darryl peeled his eyes off the envelope, noting the shaking of his hand. "Maisie."

"Yeah?" She turned back to him.

It occurred to him that Maisie cared for Penelope a great deal and coming here went against everything she believed in. That stood for something, and Darryl wouldn't forget it either. "Thanks."

Maisie gave him a sweet smile. "Welcome."

He watched her jump into her car and drive off, then he turned his attention to the letter inside the envelope.

Darryl,

I miss you. Is that weird? I mean, I know it's kinda weird since we didn't really even know each other, but I do. I miss how I felt that night with you.

Don't worry, I'm not a stalker or anything, but things are so different now. My parents divorced. That's why I had to leave so fast. It's only been six months now. They're both getting married again, and I guess I'm getting stepsiblings. Whatever that means? Truthfully, I just hope they're nice.

I don't even know why I'm writing. I don't even know if I'm going to send this. But I guess all I want to know is…will you come get me? Come bring me back to the lake, to where everything made sense, to that quiet where no one is fighting, and where life seemed so easy.

Penelope. xoxo

"YOU HAVE *GOT* to be kidding me." The police barricade was the last straw. First, Penelope's Uber driver said his car suddenly died, when she'd seen him turn off his ignition. Then the cab driver drove stupidly slow. Now *this*. It took an hour to get to the Denver airport from River Rock, and two hours had gone by now. It started to feel like she was being sabotaged.

With a huff, she got out of the car, thankfully in her winter boots, jeans, and long winter coat. "Is there a problem?" she asked the police officer standing in front of the barricade.

He wore a uniform a little different than Darryl's but had a similar matching black winter hat that she'd seen Darryl in before. "I'm sorry to report there's an accident up ahead. Road is closed."

Okay, so maybe she was overreacting, and now she felt terrible in case someone was hurt. "Is everything all right?"

"Oh, yeah, all good," another office said striding up. "There's a horse loose up there, and we gotta catch him."

Maybe she wasn't overacting at all! Penelope crossed her arms, tapping her winter boot against the snowy road. "Really? There's a car accident *and* a loose horse?"

The cops gave each other a long look, then the one on the right shrugged at her. "That's right."

"Forget this." Oh, yeah, it became pretty clear what was going on there. Darryl was pulling in favors to catch up with her on the road. Why? To voice how she disappointed him last night? Or maybe that her drunkenness had cost him his promotion? She knew she messed up, and that was exactly why she was leaving.

The last thing she wanted to do was make matters worse. She already felt like shit about it all. And all she wanted right now was to hop on that plane, get as far away from everyone as possible, and then hide under her blanket at the hotel until she had to join the cruise for training.

No one had helped her get to where she was. That

wasn't going to change today. She headed back for the cab. "Can you open the trunk?" she asked the cab driver after he rolled down the window.

"Ah, yeah, sure," the young guy said.

The trunk was open by the time she got back there, and she took out her bag, releasing the handle then dragging it along. "We're all squared up, right?" she asked as she walked by the guy again.

"Yeah, it goes on your credit card. Wait. Ma'am, where are you going?"

She was already way ahead of him. "Getting my ass to the airport myself."

When she reached the barricade again, the cop folded his arms, lifting his chest. "I can't let you do that."

"Oh, yeah? Stop me, then." He wouldn't. He couldn't.

The cop suddenly laughed softly and shook his head. "I get why Wilson's putting up such a fuss over you."

She ignored both his comment and that Darryl *had* arranged all this, and she strode past the barricade. She knew from the drive into River Rock that there was another crossroad up ahead that led to the airport. Hell, she'd hitchhike there and put all this behind her.

Yeah, right…

She internally rolled her eyes at the little voice that got her into this mess in the first place and stomped her way down the road. She shouldn't have ever let any of this happen. Now, she was a mess, feeling emotional and raw, and all the things she hated feeling. Because caring about people sucked. It was never easy.

Off in the distance, she heard sirens, making her walk just a little bit faster. Dammit. By the time she made it halfway up the hill, dragging her suitcase behind her, she was huffing and puffing and ready to keel over.

"You really need to work out more."

She gasped, spun around, and found Darryl standing behind her, with Tyson there too, wagging his tail. "It's you," she managed.

"It's me." He smiled.

Her nostrils flared as she inhaled the crisp air. "Seriously? What's wrong with you? You did all this to what? Confront me?"

"Confront you?" He snorted, shaking his head. "I told you before, when Tyson wants someone as part of their family, he'll find them. That's why we're here."

She blinked, processed, and blinked again. "But last night…"

"You got completely shitfaced." His warm gaze pinned her to the spot, as he reached into his back pocket then held up an envelope. "I'm ten years late, but I came for you." He leaned in, bringing all that heat and strength in close, stealing away the chilliness in the air, and then winked. "Even though you are a gigantic pain in my ass and wouldn't stay in one place, fighting your way to the airport, as if you thought I'd ever let you go."

She stood there a moment, thinking she could contain herself.

Then the dam opened, and there was no stopping it. She dropped her head into her hands and burst into tears.

Darryl's arms were around her in less than a second. Tight. He said nothing. She couldn't even think about talking. It felt like ten years' worth of tears got dumped right there, and for reasons unbeknownst to her, he stayed with her for all of that.

When she finally managed an ounce of control, she found her voice again, and she noticed it had begun snowing, small flakes fluttering all around them. "How did you get that letter?"

"Maisie."

"She went to your house?" she asked, surprised.

He nodded. "She loves you and wants you to be happy."

There were a thousand things to say. Questions to ask. Answers to give. But what came out was, "I'm going to mess up sometimes," she admitted. "That's what I do."

"We all mess up, Penelope. Cut yourself a break."

"Not you."

"Well, I'm perfect." He grinned.

She snorted, giving him a light tap on the arm.

He chuckled, cupping her face with his one leather-covered hand. "Of course, I mess up. I have a failed marriage in my rearview and most of the town things I'm an uptight fuddy-duddy. But that's life. And that's why I had your back last night, as did your cousins, and got you in the car before anything happened."

She felt the heat of embarrassment creep up into her face. "But I danced on the bar like an idiot."

"So what? You looked great up there. The mayor was smiling and clapping along. The captain thinks you're a saint, so nothing you could do would tarnish that."

"But I was drunk—"

"You're young. We get drunk. That's what we do." He took her by the shoulders and dropped his eyes level to hers. "And in case you think everyone is a Goodie Two-Shoes around here, don't. Mrs. Evans from the Christmas breakfast you met runs through her back yard during the full moons naked. Jason, the guy that runs the homeless shelter, was a drug addict for a long time." His mouth twitched a little when he added, "And your ever-so-perfect cousin, Clara, has had a few nights that I've driven her drunk ass home. No one is perfect, Penelope. You're a good woman. That's all that matters."

"My family…" She couldn't even get the rest of the words out.

"They hurt you, and you reacted to that hurt." He placed his arm around her neck, tugging her close, and kissed her forehead. "I've been there. I know that pain." When he leaned away, he dipped his chin and said softly, "But don't let their shit ruin you. You can't change them, but you can change how you interact with them. You've got your cousins, me"—the side of his mouth curved—"the entire town of River Rock who has fallen in love with you. Pick us. Pick here. Pick this life, not the life with people who can't see this amazing woman in front of them." He paused to wipe her tears, snowflakes covering his hair. "Ten years ago, there was a spark. One that was instant then, and lasted this past decade, always staying with me." He reached into his pocket and pulled out the mistletoe, holding it up high in between them. "Penelope Carter, will you stay and let me love you?"

"You want to love me?" Her voice cracked.

"Yeah, about that…um, I already do love you," he said, "but I can hold that in, in case that makes you want to trudge down the middle of the road again with your suitcase."

She laughed through the tears, then rose on her tip-toes. "No more running away. I love you too." She moved closer and stopped just before meeting his lips. "And just so you know, I happen to be a hundred percent certain you are not an uptight fuddy-duddy. Oh, Darryl. I can't believe you came for me."

His eyes filled with emotion. "I can't believe you kept the letter all these years." He closed the distance, pressed his mouth to hers, and kissed her, meaningfully, deeply.

Tyson barked.

Darryl broke off the kiss with a laugh.

"Oh, I won't forget about you," Penelope said, dropping down to kiss Tyson's head too.

Darryl took her suitcase in one hand, and twining the fingers of his free hand with hers, he led her back to River Rock.

Sometimes life pointed you in the wrong direction, she realized. But then sometimes it led you right to where you belonged. With a good man, a cute dog, and a very grumpy cat.

EPILOGUE

FATE FINALLY GOT things right. A week had gone by since Darryl and Tyson found Penelope trudging through the snow along the road, and she still had no little flicker in her gut telling her to hit the road. She was staying in River Rock, which was what brought her to the kitchen table with her cousins. She sat next to Maisie, glancing from face to face, hoping to hell she didn't mess up somehow. She thought back over the week, sure she hadn't done anything wrong. When their expressions revealed nothing, she broke the silence. "Okay, I know I ate the last piece of caramel apple pie, but come on, it was taunting me at two o'clock in the morning. What's a girl to do?"

Maisie giggled.

Amelia smiled.

Clara said, "That's not why we called a family meeting."

Penelope blew out a loud, relieved breath. "Okay, so what's up, then?"

Amelia turned to face Penelope fully. "I wasn't joking when I said I didn't want to do the beer tours anymore. I'm the dreamer, the creator, and I want to put my focus into creating some new beers for us to market." Amelia had graduated from the Brewmaster and Brewery Operators program in Denver.

"And I'm going on the road with our beer to try and win some of the big tasting contests," Maisie said.

Clara nodded at her sister, then said to Penelope, "You're good with people. We're all so proud of these amazing things you've done lately. So, the tour job is yours, if you want it. The pay isn't great, but you get free room and board here with us, and free dinners, of course."

Penelope parted her lips, but nothing came out, so she shut them again. She'd been wondering exactly what her next steps were. This last week had been all about heading back to the room in the Airbnb in Southern California that she'd been renting this last month and moving her stuff out to River Rock. She'd only arrived back an hour ago after Maisie picked her up from the airport since Darryl was working a shift, without much of a plan of where she would be living. "Are you all really sure about this?" she asked, a little speechless.

"Really," Clara said. "We have an extra bedroom, and who better to talk about beer and get people wanting beer, than someone who loves beer herself and is a fantastic bartender." She smiled.

Maisie grabbed Penelope's hand on the table, her eyes softening. "Say you'll take it."

Penelope didn't even have to think about it. "Of course, I'll take the job, *and* stay here with you all." Arms were suddenly surrounding her, squeals of delight filling the small kitchen. But with all this warmth around her came a reminder of something else that didn't feel quite right. "Wait." The warmth disappeared and wide eyes greeted Penelope. "Before this can happen, I need to tell you something, Clara."

"Uh-oh," Maisie said, dropping back into her seat, folding her arms.

Amelia bit her lip, obviously to hold in her laughter.

"What is it?" Clara frowned.

There couldn't be any lies between them, right? This was a new start, a fresh one. Penelope needed everything to be on the up-and-up. "Okay, so you know how I said I was *helping* Darryl with the Christmas events?"

"Yeah," Clara said, suspicion in her eyes.

Penelope cringed, wiggling in the wooden seat. "Well...it wasn't out of the goodness of my heart, per se, but because I did something that I needed to do community service for." She grabbed her phone, pulled up the video, and handed it to a very disgruntled Clara.

As the minutes dragged on, the tightness on Clara's expression slowly began to fade, and then she burst out laughing.

"Wait," Penelope gasped. "You're not mad?"

"Mad?" Clara laughed harder, rising from her seat and tucking it back under the table. "You're the one that has to live that down. That ridiculous video is punishment enough." Her laughter followed her out of the kitchen and down the hallway.

"You can stop laughing," Penelope called after her.

"No, I really can't," Clara called back.

Penelope frowned.

Amelia chuckled. "Sometimes she really does surprise the hell out of me." She gave Penelope a quick hug before leaving the kitchen.

Maisie took Amelia's place, squeezing Penelope tight. "I'm so happy you're staying. This is going to be so great, just like how it used to be during the summers."

Penelope leaned away, her eyes stinging. "I'm so happy too."

"No crying allowed," Maisie said, wiping tears from her face.

"Yes, crying is not tolerated or arrests will be made," a low voice said.

Penelope smiled, warmth immediately filling her from her head to the tips of her toes. Maisie stepped aside, revealing Darryl leaning against the doorframe, wearing and looking spectacular in his uniform. "Hi," she said.

"Welcome back."

"That's my cue," Maisie said, all but bouncing out of the kitchen. "Work starts tomorrow at nine o'clock. Don't be late or Clara *will* murder you."

"I would never let her hurt you." Darryl grinned.

"Well, good." Penelope shot to her feet and then threw her arms around his neck. "Because I have no intention of leaving any time soon."

He caught her and pulled her in close against all his hard lines. "Of course, you don't. You're home, surrounded by people who love you."

She hadn't really thought about that yet, but he was right. In his arms. In this house with her cousins. "Yeah, I'm home." And she knew now that she'd spent enough time living under the shadow of the pain and anger her parents had created. Maybe she was a memory of how their relationship failed. Or maybe she was taking the brunt of their anger toward each other. But that was on them, not her.

She refused to live under the shadow anymore.

This was *her* time for happiness, and she was taking it.

Acknowledgments

To my husband, my children, family, friends, and bestie, it's easy to write about love when there is so much love around me. Big thanks to my readers for your friendship and your support; my editor, Christa, for being the best cheerleader around; my agent, Jessica, for always having my back; the kick-ass authors in my Sprint group for their endless advice and support; Jaycee for bringing my characters to life with amazing covers, and Jolene, for making my work shine. Thank you.

About the Author

Stacey Kennedy is an outdoorsy, wine-drinking, nap-loving, animal-cuddling, USA Today bestselling romance author with a chocolate problem. She writes sexy contemporary romance full of heat and heart, including titles in her wildly hot Dangerous Love, Kinky Spurs, and Club Sin series. She lives in southwestern Ontario with her family and does most of her writing surrounded by lazy dogs.

Learn more at:
www.staceykennedy.com
Twitter @Stacey_Kennedy
Facebook.com/authorstaceykennedy
To get a FREE book, join Stacey's newsletter.
staceykennedy.com/newsletter

From USA Today Bestselling author, Stacey Kennedy comes a brand-new series, featuring a moody hero with too much baggage, a spirited heroine who is always game for adventure, and a sexy-as-hell road trip.

Check out the first book in Stacey Kennedy's
Three Chicks Brewery series . . .

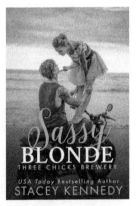

SASSY BLONDE

As the youngest Carter sister, Maisie is the free spirit of the Three Chicks Brewery, preferring to paint nature and have fun than actually show up to work. But she's determined to prove to her older sisters that she can be just as valuable to their grandfather's beer legacy as they are. Which means attending Colorado's craft brewery festivals to turn Foxy Diva, their top beer, into an award winner. Unfortunately, after more than one "beer mishap" on her own, it becomes clear to Maisie that she's going to need some help.

Enter her longtime friend, Hayes Taylor, a six-foot-three wall of hard muscle with a chip on his shoulder and a traumatic past he has no interest in working through. The last thing he needs is a woman in his life, particularly his dead wife's best friend, the sweet-as-pie Maisie, who brings out all his protective instincts. This damsel-in-distress couldn't be more Hayes's opposite, and yet, no matter how hard he tries to stay away, the cute and lively Maisie is always in his path, tempting him to want things he shouldn't.

When the two embark on a brewery festival tour, all bets are off when it comes to Hayes keeping his walls up, and Maisie feels certain she can bring her darkly brooding best friend back into the world of love and light. Hayes might have a thousand reasons to maintain his distance, but Maisie has the best reason of all for them risk their friendship and their hearts. Love.

Find out more about *Sassy Blonde*.
Stay up-to-date with Stacey's new releases and join the mailing list HERE.
staceykennedy.com/newsletter

Read on for an excerpt from the first book in Stacey Kennedy's DANGEROUS LOVE series:

NAUGHTY STRANGER

CHAPTER ONE

THE LOUD RUMBLE of the baby blue Volkswagen Beetle quieted as Peyton Kerr pressed against the brake pedal. Stoney Creek's Main Street was cute and quaint, with boutique shops lining the skinny road where cars were parked without much space in between them. Through her open window, she tasted the salt in the air coming off the Atlantic Ocean and drove by a young man packing large containers with live lobsters into the back of his old Chevy pickup. On the next corner was a ticket booth for the lighthouse boat tours. Stoney Creek was a far cry from the bright lights, skyscrapers, and pungent busy city aroma that Seattle carried, but it was also a most welcome change.

People came to Stoney Creek for the picturesque views of the coastline on the bay. They climbed the mountain that overlooked the town and the ocean. They ate fresh fish at the restaurants near the marina, walked the beaches, and sailed the open waters. Peyton came for those reasons too. Well, and a laundry list of others, including that Stoney Creek was the last vacation spot she visited with her late husband, Adam, just over a year ago. She'd been her happiest here. They swam the waters, ate too much, laughed hard enough to cry. That's what brought her back to the small Maine town. She'd left Seattle a heartbroken twenty-six-year-old widow, and she returned to Stoney Creek determined to find happiness here again.

Her heart clenched at the reminder of all she'd lost, threatening to expose all the weak spots. She forced the emotion back with a deep swallow, refusing to go to the dark place again. The past was behind her. That's where it'd stay.

Up ahead, Peyton recognized the dark-haired slender woman waiting beneath a withered store sign as Isabella, her real estate agent. Peyton squeezed her used—but new to her—car into one of the parking spots.

Before she could even get out, Isabella was already at the passenger-side door. "You made it."

"I'm so glad to finally be here." Peyton smiled, turning off the car and exiting. She'd done a nine-hour flight with a layover in Philadelphia, then landed at the Portland International Jetport. That's where she found her new car, which she thought suited small-town living. After a good night's sleep in Portland, she drove three hours, taking the scenic drive along the coast to her fresh start. "Thanks for meeting me."

"It's no problem. I've got your keys here for both

your house and your shop." Isabella reached into her purse, then handed Peyton two sets of keys. "You're all set to move in and open shop." She handed her a slew of business cards. "I've given you some names of handymen around town if you want to give the store a makeover."

Peyton glanced up at the old sign again and took in the cracked windowpane and peeling white paint on the exterior. Both the shop and her new lake house needed work, but so did she. "Great," Peyton said, feeling like a fish out of water. "Thank you so much for everything. You've been so helpful."

"Call if you need anything." Isabella smiled and, shocking Peyton, threw her arms around her like they were friends. "You're going to love it here." With a final wave, she was off, practically skipping her way down the sidewalk.

Okay, so the people were the nice, touchy-feely sort.

Peyton turned back to her new shop and exhaled the breath she hadn't known she'd been holding. Set in a historic redbrick building, in between Whiskey Blues, a jazz club on the right, and an empty store on the left, was her little lingerie shop with the French-style storefront. Two large display windows hugged the dark maple door with the original brass handle. The store might not be much in size, but the charm of the shop made up for it.

It was also 100 percent hers. Paid for with the insurance money from Adam's death. Two weeks ago, in her lowest of lows, a Facebook ad for the Stoney Creek B&B, where she and Adam had stayed at when they'd vacationed there, had popped up on her screen. After that, she'd fallen down the Internet hole until she discovered the local lingerie shop was for sale. Everything from there happened so fast; she'd up and bought the shop on a total whim. Because if anything could make her feel happy again, it would be found in the place she felt the happiest. She also kept thinking that if she could make other women feel beautiful, then she'd feel that way again too.

This past year, she had no reason to wear gorgeous lingerie, let alone find a reason to get out of bed. She wore cotton bras and underwear for comfort. But she'd had a blast selling lingerie during her nursing school days. She couldn't help but think that buying a lingerie shop was a good step forward to finding the fun parts of herself that had disappeared with Adam's death.

Sure, she knew her mental state was hanging in the balance of her new life and her new shop. She couldn't fail. Not because of the money. Adam had left her in good shape financially. But she couldn't fail because this was *all* she had. There nothing else giving her a purpose. And she was done playing the victim. She was also done simply surviving. She'd already been doing that in spades in Seattle. She wanted to breathe. To *live*.

And that's why she'd left Seattle and her parents.

She'd given up her nursing career in the ER at Seattle's General Hospital, and she'd dumped every cent she received from Adam's insurance money into this shop and her little house on the lake.

Was she crazy?

Oh, yeah, she was totally batshit nuts.

She glanced down at the house keys in her hand. All of her belongings would be shipped tomorrow, so tonight she planned to stay at the Stoney Creek B&B a couple blocks down Main Street.

"Are you the new owner?"

Peyton turned around, finding an older couple smiling at her. "Yes, I am."

"Oh, so lovely to hear," the woman said, her arm wrapped in her husband's. "We need more young business owners coming in and keeping our downtown alive." She offered her hand. "I'm Marjorie, and this is Joe."

Peyton returned Marjorie's handshake and then shook Joe's hand. "It's nice to meet you both. I'm Peyton." When she drew her hand away, her stomach suddenly rumbled *loudly*. "I'm sorry about that. Apparently, I'm starving."

Joe's amber eyes crinkled with his warm smile. "The bar next door has one of the best fish sandwiches in town."

"That sounds delicious." Peyton returned the smile,

feeling the tightness in her chest begin to dissolve. "I'll be sure to check it out. Thanks."

"Enjoy your evening, Peyton," Marjorie said. With a final wave, they continued on their walk.

When Peyton's stomach growled again, she headed for the bar, thinking a drink along with food sounded like the next best step forward. She didn't see any parking signs, figuring she could leave her car there for the night.

She grabbed her purse from the car, locked the doors and entered the bar. From its original flagstone walls and restored burgundy velvet chairs to the gold accents, the bar was pure class. Four large crystal chandeliers gave the space a warm, inviting feel, and round tables surrounded the black shiny stage, where a man had his head bowed over the piano he played.

Peyton headed for the bar that had three men drinking beers. She hastily moved to the other side, keeping her distance from anyone of the opposite sex. Even the *hot* guy with the dark hair and muscular biceps who held her gaze, the side of his mouth curving sensually. Actually, *especially* because of that. She needed to find herself again, not find herself in anyone's bed.

When she slid onto the stool, a friendly voice said, "You're new here."

Peyton glanced up, finding a slim, long-haired brunette wearing a black T-shirt that read whiskey blues across her chest. The bright pink lipstick she wore made her big blue eyes pop.

"Yup, I'm brand spanking new." Peyton smiled, offering her hand. "I bought the store next door."

"Did you?" The woman returned the handshake. "Well, that makes us friends already, then."

Peyton laughed. "And here I was thinking making new friends was going to be hard." She placed her hands back onto her purse. "I'm Peyton."

"Kinsley," the woman said, grabbing a martini glass. "Lucky for you, I own this place, which means I can call it a night and celebrate us being neighbors." She gestured at the glass. "Chocolate martinis sound okay?"

"Sounds divine," Peyton said, her mouth watering. She definitely wanted a fish sandwich, but a little liquid love first didn't hurt. Besides, she hoped the drink would help dissolve the lump in her throat. She questioned her sanity, uprooting her life and leaving her family behind. But she couldn't have stayed in Seattle another day. Seattle belonged to her and Adam. She needed to belong without him. Adam was gone. He wasn't coming back.

Kinsley finished pouring two glasses, then held hers up. "To new friendships and new beginnings."

Peyton lifted her glass. "Cheers to that!"

Before long, one glass turned into two glasses, and Peyton's belly felt warm, her smile easy, the fish sandwich long forgotten. She spoke of Seattle, leaving out all the personal parts, keeping those secrets locked up tight. And Kinsley shared life in Stoney Creek, the fun places to go, the sights to see.

"I make a damn fine martini," Kinsley said, licking the chocolate flakes off her upper lip. She placed her empty glass behind the bar. "Give me a couple minutes, then we'll Uber it to this new house of yours on the lake and grab some takeout on the way. I gotta see this place. It sounds amazing."

Sure, Kinsley was a stranger, but something about her laidback way put Peyton at ease. "Deal." Peyton took another sip of her drink, watching Kinsley leave the bar and move into the back room, feeling happier than she'd felt in an entire year.

Something warm suddenly brushed against Peyton's arm, making her shiver. She turned as Mr. Crooked Smile sat on the stool next to her. He was tall—around six foot two, pure muscle, an all-around fine specimen of a man. His intense blue eyes that appeared nearly gray in the low lighting held hers, and his five-o'clock shadow brought her attention to his totally kissable lips. He wore a navy-blue T-shirt that stretched across his chest, showcasing hard biceps, and jeans that hugged his thick thighs.

"Hi." He grinned, voice as smooth as melted chocolate. And she really liked chocolate. A lot.

She took in the hard masculine lines of his face,

softened a little by the strands of dark hair falling across his forehead. "I'm new here, opening the shop next door," she babbled.

"Ah, the lingerie shop," he said, his eyes dancing at whatever was crossing her expression. "Tonight's a celebration, then?"

God, she must have *looked* like she wanted to eat him. Well, she *did*, so whatever. Obviously, the martinis without food had been a terrible idea. "That's right," she said, lifting her chin, trying not to look as rattled by this guy or as tipsy as she felt.

His arm brushed against hers again—clearly intentional this time—and she shivered, hearing her own hitching breath. His gaze went *red hot*, those deep eyes turning darker, examining her deeper. She swallowed, trying to calm her puckering nipples and the building heat between her thighs.

What. The. Hell?

"Um, excuse me." She slid off the stool and stumbled in the process. After she laughed at herself and hid her gaze from him, she beelined it toward the bathroom across the bar. Once inside, she turned on the water and placed her hands underneath to cool off. She looked into the mirror, finding her cheeks flushed, her eyes glossy and full of heat. Maybe those chocolate martinis had an aphrodisiac effect. Because . . . *holy hell!*

She stayed in the bathroom probably longer than

necessary. When she came out, she nearly walked into Mr. Crooked Smile. He caught her by the waist to steady her, and when his hands tightened on her hips something overcame her, an emotion she could not control. His touch was warm and strong, and his potent stare pulled her in until she looked into his eyes intimately.

He arched an eyebrow. "All right?"

"Why are you waiting here for me?" she managed.

His smile was gentle and sweet, and on a big tough guy looked mouthwateringly delicious. "You've been in there a while. Feeling okay?"

She stared at him. For some reason she was immensely touched by his kindness, and she suddenly couldn't remember all the reasons she didn't want a man in her life. "God, you're so hot." She grabbed his face and kissed him. Passionately. With tongue.

A low masculine sound that tickled her in the best places rose from deep in his chest. Then her back hit the wall. Hard. Shock and desire flooded her as he threaded one hand into her hair, then claimed her mouth. Owned it, with every hard press of his lips and swirl of his tongue.

When she began nearly climbing up his body, a moment of clarity hit her, and she broke away with a gasp. "What in the hell are we doing?" she asked, staring at his mouth, and wanting desperately to have more of it. "You're a stranger." *A naughty stranger.*

"I believe you kissed me," he said in a voice so low goose bumps rose on her arms, and a smile so sexy it should come with a warning label. "And were doing a fine job of it."

"Ahem."

Still in the man's arms, Peyton turned, finding Kinsley staring at them with her arms folded.

"So," Kinsley said with a sly smile. "I see you've met my brother, Boone."

Find out more about *Naughty Stranger.*
Stay up-to-date with Stacey's new releases and join the mailing list HERE.
staceykennedy.com/newsletter

CPSIA information can be obtained
at www.ICGtesting.com
Printed in the USA
LVHW112147041219
639495LV00002B/534/P